Beth,

Why choose?

Dani ♡

René xo

Vengeance of
THE FALLEN

TWISTED LEGENDS COLLECTION

DANI RENÉ

Author's
NOTE

Dear Reader,

I'm so excited to have you reading my first ever
reverse harem romance. It's been one hell of a
journey.

Please note, there are dark elements in this story,
and there may be triggers which could upset
sensitive readers. Please be wary when diving in.
If you'd like a full list of triggers, please click this
link:
https://danirene.com/book/vengeance-of-the-fallen

Mad love,
Dani, xo

Welcome...

Ten authors invite you to join us in the
Twisted Legends Collection.

These stories are a dark, twisted reimagining of
infamous legends well-known throughout the
world. Some are retellings, others are nods to those
stories that cause a chill to run down your spine.

Each book may be a standalone, but they're
all connected by the lure of a legend.

We invite you to venture into the unknown,
and delve into the darkness with us,
one book at a time.

The
COLLECTION

Dedication

To my girls who hate to choose.

Playlist

Animals - Maroon 5
The Devil Within - Digital Daggers
Black Sun - Blue Oyster Cult
River - Bishop Briggs
Stalker - J See, Azide, Lox Chatterbox, Black Tash
Drive You Insane - Daniel Di Angelo
See You Bleed - Ramsey
Desire - Violet Orlandi
Miss You - CORPSE
White Tee - CORPSE
Flesh - Simon Curtis
Saints - Echos
Ritual - AWAY, Echos
Nothing At All - Rob Dougan

Find the full playlist on Spotify

Preface
CROW

NOBODY STARTS THEIR LIFE OUT AS A KILLER. No child wakes up one morning and announces he's going to become a hitman.

But that's where life has brought me. It's in the eyes of my brothers in arms I find my humanity. If you can even call it that.

We've all three witnessed atrocities, and when we watched these violent acts unfolding, it wasn't on a television screen, it was real life. Perhaps it's why my mind broke. I'm certain it's why Falcon and Hawk, my brothers by all standards that matter, hunger for the same revenge that I need.

We may not be blood, but we're family all the same.

They are the only people I trust with my life.

Because they know how precious it is. Being alive, it's a gift, one that can be taken at any moment. It has brought us to the work we do. We know how to steal those last moments of someone's light and snuff it out as if they'd never existed.

Most people who know us, fear us—and they should.

We can empty your bank account, find every dark, sordid secret you've ever had hidden away, and we'll do it so we can get our payday. When your life is gone, there is no getting it back. Most times, we don't have to kill those we're hired to because once we're done they want to die anyway.

It makes our lives much easier.

Wealthy people hire us to do their dirty work, and I don't mind. I like to get my hands filthy. There's honesty in what I do. With a swipe of my blade, with the pull of a trigger, I can take out anyone who stands in my way.

There is only one person who I haven't killed yet, and it's not for the lack of trying. He's locked up tight in prison. I know he'll get out; he has connections. One day, and I know the day will come, I'll look him in the eye and watch the life drain from his face.

I want to bathe in his blood. It will be sweet vengeance.

In the darkness of the living room, I move to

the balcony with a cigarette pressed between my lips. Outside, I flick the lighter and take a long, deep inhale. It's as if I can *see* the smoke curling around my nerves, collecting in my lungs, and when I breathe it out, it billows like a cloud.

The apartment is draped in darkness, and I blend into my surroundings, dressed all in black as I stand guard. My watchful gaze is trained on the building across from me. I can see her moving around her flat. She's oblivious to me. But she'll soon learn danger lurks in the shadows.

Each night I come to the apartment we bought in the city only to watch her. This is our ticket to the one thing we've been wanting for years. At first, Falcon was concerned about my plan, but when I told him she's the spawn of the most evil man we'd ever come across, he agreed.

I kept her a secret for months before I told my brothers. Something I have never done before. They know everything there is to know about me. I can't explain it, but there is something about her I want to keep to myself. A piece of her which calls to me.

A pretty little blonde with angel eyes and pouty lips. Her body is sinful. Perhaps it's the reason why I didn't tell my brothers. Because I know the moment Falcon sees her, he'll want to enjoy every curve.

My blood heats as she moves to the second bedroom of her apartment where she'll log into her computer, touch herself, and come. Her orgasm will be real, and she'll slowly come down from her high. But deep down the guilt will eat away at her like it does every time she does it. I watch the way she rushes from the room afterward. It happens at least twice a week. She'll run to the main bedroom, cover herself in a robe, and curl up on a chair by the window as tears streak her cheeks.

Our Goldilocks is broken in ways I didn't fathom. I had no idea what was going on the first few times it happened. It doesn't stop my need to make her pay. Even if she begs for her life, she owes me one back. And I intend on taking.

I know who she really is.

I know what she did.

Prologue
LUCILLE

Five Years Ago

"**G**UILTY." *GUILTY. GUILTY.* The word rings in my ears, over and over again. A deafening thud of a gavel hitting the wooden surface of the judge's desk makes me jump in surprise. Everything spins as if I'm on a carnival ride and it's going too fast. *He* turns to look at me; the man who's being convicted of murder. The sneer curling his lips has ice crawling up my spine, one icicle at a time. The venom dancing in his eyes threatens to poison me right where I sit.

I did this.

My world tilts on its axis when he lifts his finger to his nose and taps it three times. It used to be our *thing*, but I no longer want any connection to the stranger before me. My knees wobble as I try to push to my feet. I can feel the bile rising from my stomach, the burn traveling hot and fast up my throat.

I race from the courtroom as the tears stream from my eyes. Thankfully, I make it into a stall in the ladies' restroom before I puke up my breakfast. I told my mother I didn't want anything to eat, and yet, she made me have something.

My body continues convulsing as I cry. It's not sadness overtaking me, it's the sense of foreboding. He will come for me. I don't doubt he will find a way out and when he does, I'll be his next victim. There was no longer a question about it. It's a given. That's how my life will end.

"Lucy?" My mother's voice echoes outside the stalls. "Where are you?"

"I'm here," I croak, my throat burns from the acid I expelled.

She doesn't say anything for a long while. We didn't expect this to happen. I never wanted my family to be broken up by heartbreak or disaster, but here we are. The confusion running through me when my father was arrested is still present.

I haven't come to terms with it.

I want to; but admitting your father is a killer isn't the kind of painful truth any child should have to come to terms with—even if he claimed he'd lost his mind; he wasn't thinking straight. I can't forgive him for what he did.

"Come, Lucy girl," Mother calls to me. "We should go." She's right. But my strength is gone. My arms shake as I attempt to push myself to my feet. By the time I open the door to the stall, my mother looks at me with tears shining in her eyes.

"I'm sorry."

"You have nothing to be sorry for." It's the same thing she tells me every day. Well, since *that* fateful day. But I don't believe her. I feel as guilty as he is. My gut churns as I rinse my mouth and splash some cool water on my face.

It's the silence hanging over us as we make our way home which reminds me of what we lost. The happy memories are all gone, and all we have left in their wake are images of horror.

When we reach the house where my father lived, it feels as if I'm a stranger. Fear laced with darkness hangs in every room, even my bedroom. The memories of what happened in here assault me. I should have run. Perhaps one day I'll have the courage to walk away from my mother and leave her, but now, after he's gone, I can't abandon her.

She knew about what was going on. She knew my father was a criminal, and she didn't do anything. As much as I want to hate her, I can't. Fear makes people do things they normally wouldn't.

Knowing your husband is working for criminals, for a dangerous organization which can kill you with a flick of their fingers, it forces you to stay silent.

I thought long and hard about my testimony. They asked me questions I'd rather not answer, but I was under oath.

Did your father ever hurt you?

Did he ever tell you to do anything you didn't want to?

Did you witness him ever touch or force any of the victims?

All those words, those fucking questions, brought back those dark nights when I thought I would sleep and I couldn't. When you live with someone who's an expert at pretending, you can't fool them.

As I walk into my bedroom, it's as if he's still here, waiting for me. I can practically envision him on my bed, holding my teddy bear while asking me to strip. There is one memory I buried so deep I didn't want to think about it until now.

The mattress has a dent where he used to lay. The chair which overlooks my bed still has an imprint of where he would sit while reading me stories. Most children want their folks to tell them bedtime tales of princesses and heroes, and knights in shining armor.

I didn't.

It was the worst time of my life.

Each night he would come into my bedroom and relay the story about the princess who needed so much more than anyone else could give her.

He would tell me how she begged the dragon to take her, to steal her away and keep her locked in a tower where they would play games all day. I was much younger and trying to understand why he was telling me these things, and it was only on my fifteenth birthday I realized the truth.

There was so much more to the story than meets the eye. You wouldn't know it until it was explained in fine detail. As the princess, I wanted more. The attention he gave me made me happy, but it wasn't the right kind. I didn't realize until the night he made sure I knew what a monster he was.

Then it was too late to refuse it. He said he would hurt me worse than him stealing my purity, if I told him no. I tried to fight back, which was when he told me I would regret it because I would be labeled as the problem. At the time, I believed him. I didn't want people to think of me as a liar, so I allowed it to happen.

Even when I wanted to cry.

Even when I begged him to stop.

He didn't. There was no longer a right or wrong in his eyes. Everything he did was for the greater good. He told me it would all make sense when I was older. He was convinced what he was doing was right. Later I learned about his connection to the vile criminals he worked for, and a light shone on the dark memories which plagued me.

The night before I learned of his true intentions, he said he would make sure nobody would get the one part of me men craved. I knew what he meant because I'd overheard girls at school talking.

I was never allowed out with boys.

My father told me I was special. For a long time, I believed him.

But I wasn't.

All he saw when he looked at me was a chess piece. He moved me around, toyed with me, and used me up until there were no more moves left. I was promised. My life would become nothing more than a bargaining chip which my father used to ensure his safety.

He didn't care I would be sent off with a man twice or three times my age.

He laughed at the thought. Because he would have taken a girl my age and enjoyed it. The men he worked with didn't care about much, especially how young the women, or girls, were when they bought and sold them.

A bartering deal between dangerous devils.

While girls were the currency.

I flop on the bed as I recall every vile memory.

It's like a movie reel playing in my mind. It repeats, over and over again. Images flash across my eyelids, like a large screen, bright and telling. It spews a story filled with lies.

Tears and pleas.

Grunts and moans.

Even as pain took hold, the princess begged to stop feeling, to leave this earth. She wanted nothing more than to escape, but the dragon held her hostage. She could run, perhaps find solace with three bears who would love her endlessly. Or she could find a prince with a red rose dying slowly as he lost his own life.

But none of those were real.

Those girls were nothing more than fabrications in the minds of authors. Real life is nothing like those books. I used to flick the pages excitedly. I knew soon after falling in love with books, my story wouldn't end with a happily ever after.

I would be devoured by the monster.

I would be captured by the villain.

Now, as exhaustion takes a hold of me, I know my dragon has been slayed, but he'll be back to find me.

It doesn't matter how long it takes.

One
LUCILLE

Present Day

FRUSTRATION BURNS THROUGH ME AS I PICK UP MY CELL phone and log into my social media accounts. Photos of the parties happening on summer break annoy me. My friends are out having fun while my mother forces me to work this part time job.

Sighing, I leave my phone on the sofa before heading into the kitchen. I can't be angry at her though. She's a single mom who needs to put food on the table. She does her best for me, and I know it. I'm sour-faced because I know I could be out there enjoying my birthday if my father wasn't such a weasel.

Nothing more than a waste of space, he walked out when I was ten. I remember his face each time he needed *to go to work. It was his excuse. My mother was already doing double shifts at the hospital when he walked out, and I was left to my own devices while she worked.*

Which brings me to the present day, six years later, and I'm earning my own money, it's not a lot. There's a sense of independence when you realize you can buy anything you want, you have to put the hours in. I think back to the times I spent hours in the garden back in our small town, and I wonder what would have happened had my mother not taken the job offer in the city.

The shit hole I grew up in is now nothing more than a memory. Mom's job brought us to the City of Angels — Los Angeles. She didn't want to leave Holbrook, but we needed to get out of the one horse town.

I open the fridge to find an array of delicacies stacked high on the shelves. Our home isn't as lavish as this one, but we do all right. I pick out some strawberries and a cola before settling back on the sofa.

Thankfully, the kids have turned in for the night. The Hendersons have been good to me, and tonight, they promised to pay me double since their eldest son is back from college and they're taking him out. I never met him, but I'm sure he's spoiled from what I've seen the twins have.

Suddenly, the landline buzzes loudly, breaking the monotonous mumbling from the television, causing me to jump. It hardly ever rings. But the Hendersons sometimes have clients call, which they mentioned may happen. Mr.

Henderson told me it's linked to his office which means it could be something important.

I pick it up with a fake smile on my face. "Hello, the Hendersons," I greet. There's silence in response, and I wonder if whoever it was hung up, but when I'm about to hang up, I hear breathing. The sound has the hairs on the back of my neck standing on end.

"Hello, little sitter." A deep, raspy voice comes through the line sending ice through my veins. I glance at the television and have to suppress my giggle. It has to be one of my friends playing around since I'm watching some stupid teen horror movie.

My heart thuds against my ribs and my stomach twists with fear. "Who is this?"

"The kids are in danger, little sitter," the stranger whispers, and it's as if I can feel his hot breath against my skin causing my stomach to convulse as acid climbs up to my throat.

"Stop being an asshole," I bite out, but laugh when I hear the deep breathing. "Josh, is that you?" Silence greets me back, and fear slowly snakes its way through my veins. "Josh?" But even as I whisper his name, I know it's not him. Call it intuition, but my gut tells me the person on the other end of the line is some fucked up weirdo.

"Get out of the house because I'm coming for them, little sitter," the voice says, and I'm sure I'm dreaming. Or having a nightmare because this can't be real. Things like this only happen in movies. I want to laugh, to call

this person's bluff, but something deep in my gut tells me not to.

"Who is this?" I ask again, this time, fear hits me right in the gut.

"They will die, and you can't stop it," he says, and for a moment, I think I recognize the deep gravely tone. I almost want to call out and say Dad, but I don't because he left. He doesn't know where we are. Also, why would he try to scare me.

"Listen, I don't know what game—"

A crash comes from upstairs and I drop the phone, racing up the steps to the second floor where I find the stairwell window shattered into a million pieces. On the floor at my feet is a brick. The dark red confirms it's from the garden maze where the kids play.

"Shit." I turn left and head for the twins' bedroom. They're asleep when I rush into the room. I shake them both. "Wake up," I call out to them, panic rises in my chest as a continuous thud echoes from out in the hallway.

"What's happening?"

"Get up. Quickly," I bite out as frustration takes a hold of me. We can't go out into the hallway, so I push both sleepy boys into the bathroom and shut the door behind me. They haven't realized the fear in my stance yet since they're both barely awake, and I pray they don't see it because I've never been so afraid before.

I check my pockets and realize I left my phone on the sofa. "Shit."

"Shit?"

"Don't say that," I tell Anwar who looks as confused as his brother. I've been looking after them for a couple of months. I've never had an intruder in the house before — in any of the homes I've sat in — so this has me panicking.

"What's — ?" His question is thwarted by the crashing of items in the bedroom, and I have to pull the boys into my arms as we sink to the floor. Tears race down my cheeks, both kids are shaking against me, and all I can do is pray whoever the fuck is in the house doesn't make it to this door.

My heart thuds against my chest, the deafening rhythm thrumming in my ears. Over the noise from outside the bathroom, I breathe deeply, but it does nothing to calm my erratic pulse.

As much as I know we're sitting ducks if we don't try to get away, there's nowhere to go since we're on the second floor. If we even tried climbing from the window, we'll fall to our death. Either way, we're fucked.

Both boys look up at me through wet lashes, and I wish I could stop whatever is about to happen, but I can't. Instead, I pull their heads down, lowering my own and closing my eyes.

The thudding from the bedroom stops, and silence hangs heavily around us, but something tells me it's not over. The threat is close. I have never prayed, ever, but right now, in this bathroom, I do. I silently call out to a man in the clouds to keep us safe and get us through this.

I've seen all the movies. I've even laughed at them. It's always the babysitter who gets killed in the end. My stomach drops when I hear the door handle twisting. The door is locked, but I doubt it will stop whoever wants to get in.

The boys tremble in my arms, and I wonder if we can make a getaway through the adjoining room. Thankfully, their folks decided it would be a good idea to have their rooms on either side of the bathroom.

I shoo them toward the opposite door, and we slowly, silently make our way there, but the moment we're over the threshold, something grabs at my hair and shoves me back, causing me to stumble into the wall with a painful thud.

"No!" My throat burns with the screech as I watch the man in black make his way toward the boys. My back aches, it feels as if something is broken, but I rush to the bedroom where he turns and glares at me with black eyes.

He's wearing a mask, so I can't see his face, but the venom in his glare is enough to stop me in my tracks. The glint of a blade has my heart leaping into my throat.

"Don't hurt them," I plead, hoping he'll leave the kids alone. They're barely ten years old. And they're good boys. They've never given me trouble while I've watched them.

The man in black laughs a deep, throaty chuckle before turning and grabbing one of them by his hair. The other tries to fight, but it's no use. I grab a lamp from the *nightstand and race to where the intruder is, but he's fast. He spins on his heel and the sleek, metal slices through my clothes and blood oozes from my stomach.*

When his gaze falls to the wound, he turns, grabs both boys, and rushes from the house as I fall to my knees. I have to get to a phone.

"No!" I cry out, but it's too late because he's gone. On my hands and knees, I crawl through the room to the hallway, leaving a trail of crimson in my path. By the time I reach the living room, I'm weakened by the loss of blood. Just then, the front door swings open and all I hear are voices.

Darkness clouds my vision and I know it's no longer possible for me to keep my eyes open. As the pain sears through my body, I allow sleep to take me.

"Are you okay?" A deep rumble comes from beside me, and a scream tears itself from my throat. The burning sensation causing me to cough.

When I open my eyes, I find kind, but worried eyes beside me. He looks at me as if I've lost my mind. I'm pretty sure I have. But I can't tell him the truth. I can never confess I am scared of becoming like my father.

"I'm fine," I tell him. It's a lie. Everything he knows about me is a lie. He's handsome, caring, and I know he loves me, but I can never truly be with him. I'm nothing more than a liar, and he doesn't deserve it. "Perhaps you should go."

"What?" The shock in his tone is clear. "It's two in the fucking morning, Becs," he says, calling me the name I gave him. "Becs, what is happening?" The concern in his tone cracks through my chest, reminding me of why I'm doing this. I should never have said yes when he asked me out. But the loneliness got to me.

I focused on my life, my secrets, and one night stands were all I ever allowed myself until Roger walked into the bar where I work. He wore me down and now I have to hurt him.

"Get out." I don't look at him as I pull on my clothes. "Get out. I need you out." My hands tremble as I shrug on a hoodie. The cold has taken over me, and I shiver as I the memories still plague me.

"Becs," Roger coos, but I can't do this. "Please, why are you doing this? You know I—"

"I said get the fuck out of my apartment!" This time, I turn and glare at the man who's tried to be good to me. We've been dating for three months. In the time he's been with me, I've really tried, but he started talking about marriage and kids, and then the nightmares returned.

"Fuck," Roger grunts as he dresses quickly, but I can feel his angry stare on me. He makes one more attempt before he walks out. "Are you okay?"

"Just leave."

I stand in the darkness for a long time.

I don't expect anyone to understand. Maybe I'm as broken as my father, and as shattered as my mother. There's no hope for me. I don't expect anyone else to love me this way.

A knock on the door grabs my attention and I want to shout at Roger to leave, but with a sigh, I make my way to tell him once again it's over. I pull open the door, expecting to see his worried stare, but instead, on the welcome mat is a bunch of tulips. They're a soft pink color, but what alarms me is the red spray they're covered in.

I pick up the vase and I find a note. The stench of metal is apparent. It's not red paint; it's blood. The vase falls from my hand, hitting the tiles with a loud crash. Glass shards cut into my bare feet, but I don't feel anything other than the swirling in my head.

With trembling fingers, I open the note, and the breath is knocked from my lungs.

A little liar, hidden in plain sight. We know who you are and we're coming... soon.

It's probably the long white-blonde hair hanging to the middle of her back. Or it's the soft hazel eyes she pierces through our armor with because they seem to shine like sunshine through a storm. If I were a hero, I would want to save her. But I'm the villain in her story.

I want nothing more than to see her cry.

To watch her cheeks turn red as she sobs for mercy.

I don't show sympathy.

It's been a long time since that word has been associated with me. I pull the black hoodie up over my head to cover most of my face and I turn away from her laughing face. The more happiness I see in her expression, the hotter my blood burns.

Our sleek matte black Ferraris sit waiting for us as we reach them hidden in the lot behind some trees. I slip into the driver's seat of mine, and Falcon knocks on the blacked out glass. Rolling my eyes, I lower the window and look at him.

"What?"

"We need to meet at the house," he tells me. "If this is going to go down, everything needs to be ready for her." I would tell him I don't give a fuck, but I would be lying. The cage we have for our little Goldilocks has to be tamper proof. She can't be trusted.

"Fine." I turn on the engine and pull out of

the lot with a squeal of tires. The rhythmic thump of heavy bass from "The Devil Within" by Digital Daggers emanates from the speakers.

My thoughts go to her as the lyrics fill my senses, and I smile. It's been a long time coming. The sitter needs to pay for her father's sins.

I grab the packet of smokes from my pocket and press one between my lips. The flame of the lighter dances in the cool breeze, but I manage to light up the cigarette. I pull in a lungful of smoke which slowly calms my erratic heartbeat.

Each time I see her, it's the same. My reaction to the beauty is nothing more than anger, but I can't deny she's exquisite. If she weren't our mark, I'd have fucked her over and over again until her body was nothing more than a mess of sated limbs and a soft smile.

Groaning, I shift in my seat, trying to focus on the road instead of my hardening cock. It's been a while since I got my dick wet. Perhaps I should head out tonight and get lost in a few women before we bring in little Lucy. I can't lose control around her. The mouse who's going to live in the mansion, haunted by the memories of what her father did to us.

He may not have hurt us, but his actions caused the chaos we now live with. My mother, Falcon's father, and Hawk's uncle and aunt are all shattered beyond belief. Lucille doesn't get to live a happy life while ours are drenched in darkness.

I glance at my rear-view mirror to see Falcon behind me. I'm certain Hawk is following. We tend to go out in threes. We hunt the way we fuck. Together. They're my best friends and have been since we were kids. Since we left L.A. to move to the small town in the countryside across the pond, we've become closer than I ever imagined.

There has always been a connection between us. But it became something more a few years ago. My folks know nothing about the life I now lead. It helps I'm not in contact with them. But it's no fault of my own. When they lost the twins, they changed. I needed to escape the grief which had taken a hold on my family, and it's brought me to a place where me and my brothers can now be free.

Not everyone accepts the lifestyle we lead, but I'm happy here. Or as happy as can be because there is still the little problem I have—the need to kill Mahoney. When I think about him and what he did to my family, I can't help but experience the blood lust burning me from the inside out.

It's the same with Falcon and Hawk. We all went through similar pain, and it is something which has connected us on levels I didn't expect. Yes, we came together in our agony, but we built it into an empire.

Our heartbreak and pain brought us to a place

where we can enjoy what we have left in our lives. It brought us to the small town of Lakeside. We are well known in these parts as The Fallen. We do the jobs wealthy bastards hire us for so they don't have to get their hands dirty.

I play with my knives, while Falcon enjoys fire. But Hawke, he's the quiet killer. He uses his hands, which is why they're usually bandaged as if he only moments ago got out of the ring. An ex-MMA fighter, he's found his calling in vengeance alongside us.

My cell phone rings on the Bluetooth speaker putting a stop to my music. When I cast a quick glance at the screen, I notice my mother's name across the screen. She decided to continue her life in the City of Angels. She's only there wishing her baby would return. Not me, I haven't been under her wing since I turned thirteen. At thirty I can't imagine still living with her.

"Mom," I greet when I answer the call.

"Cordon—"

"You know my name is Crow," I bite out, gritting my teeth when she uses my real name. I haven't been called by my real name in years, which is why I usually ignore her calls.

"Oh, please," she mumbles. "I wanted to see you. I'm thinking of coming to Lakeside for Christmas," she informs me. At least it gives me two months to prepare.

"Okay," I say slowly, waiting for the kicker. My mother doesn't call to make small talk. Everything she does has a reason behind it. Her visiting means there has been a development in the company she took over for me. Also, she wants me to give this plan of vengeance up and go home.

"I was thinking perhaps you'd like to look over the books for your father's business," she announces, but her voice is filled with nerves. She's been trying to get me to take over my father's business since he had a heart attack and left everything to her, but I've refused time and again.

She knows I don't want it. I never have. I'm not made for it, and I'm most definitely not made for suits.

"Please, son," she pleads like she always does. As bad as I feel letting her down, I can't bring myself to care about stocks and shares. The job I have now pays well; I don't even have to work if I don't want to. My father also made sure both her and I were looked after. After my twin brothers were murdered, he doted on me and Mom. We were his life and when he died, we were left with so much fucking money, we could probably use it as toilet paper and still never run out.

"I'm driving," I tell her suddenly. "I'll call you later." I hang up before she can whine about not having anything to do, before she can ask about me walking into the offices of Brandt and Associates and taking my father's seat. I can't deal with the guilt trip she likes to play on my emotions with right now.

I pull up to the enormous gun-metal gates leading to The Fallen mansion. Even when I left L.A., I knew I would be with my brothers forever. We may not be blood, but we're bound by revenge. It's stronger than any genetic link could be.

Exiting the car, I turn to find Falcon already making a beeline for the house. When Hawk joins me, he chuckles. "The bastard got a call."

"And?"

"The little mouse may have another stalker besides us. We were on a call when his phone went mental," he tells me as we make our way into the house.

We rush through the entrance and into Falcon's office before I have time to consider what the fuck this means. I know her father is locked up tight, and there is no way he's getting out without us being informed. That's what money gets you—loyalty from the law.

"What the fuck is going on?" I demand before Hawk can say anything more.

Falcon's gaze is glued to the screen as he clicks through what I can only assume are documents of information. I leave the tech shit to him. I, on the other hand, don't mind getting my hands dirty.

"I think we may have a problem," he murmurs as he continues reading. "The info I pulled on Lucille has been accessed by someone else. It's not the feds, and it's definitely not any of our contacts."

"Find out who the fuck it is." The order comes swiftly. We're the only people who can fuck her life up. Nobody else has that privilege. We've earned it. We've waited years for it, and now we have her in our sights, I'm not letting her slip through my fucking fingers.

"I'm going to do a deep dive now," Falcon tells me as he settles in for a night of work. "Bring me something to eat when you get there."

"I'm not your fucking maid," I bite out, but laugh when he gives me a look which tells me if he doesn't do this hack, I'll have to. "Yeah, okay, don't whine about it." Rolling my eyes in frustration, I sigh. We've always been lighthearted in our banter with each other. But we also know there are times to be serious. I'm not like this with anyone else. Not even my own family.

"You two should get married," Hawk mumbles as he shakes his head and walks out of the office, and I follow. Our home is far too big for the three of us, but we have our own space, even while being close.

"I don't like this," I tell him. "When new fuckers come on the scene, it sets me on edge."

"You're always on fucking edge, Crow," Hawk informs me coolly as we make our way into the kitchen. In the fridge, I find some meals already made by our chef. We have a few staff on hand over the course of the week, and on weekends they go home to their families with a pay packet to ensure they return the following Monday.

"Fuck you," I bite out, but he's right. I'm on edge because we finally have her in our sights. I have been following her for a couple of weeks. We had to learn her schedule, and I took it upon myself to stalk her, making sure she didn't run. But the girl doesn't notice me around, which is how I like it. As much as she should be alert, I've realized she's as oblivious to her surroundings as we are aware of ours.

Hawk grips the back of my neck and holds me steady. "Listen to me," he speaks, slow and calm. "It's going to work out." He's been a constant in my life for a long time. I can't imagine my life without him or Falcon. Before I can respond, he pulls me close and presses his lips to mine. It's nothing more than a quick kiss, but it calms me somewhat.

When I first realized I was bi, I struggled with it. At times, I still do. But being on my own, living without the watchful eyes of my parents, I've been able to explore my sexuality more than I did when I was younger. Since I've finally given in to my instinct, what comes naturally to me, I can accept who I am.

"Falcon is going to be busy for the rest of the night. I'll make sure dinner is ready for everyone to eat when they want," Hawk says as he stalks off to the pantry where there are ready-made meals waiting for us.

He's the only one of the three of us who enjoys being in the kitchen. He even spends time in here while Marta is here cooking up a storm. We leave him to it. He once mentioned it's therapeutic. What I find calming is far from being in the fucking kitchen standing at in front of a cooker all day.

"I'm going upstairs," I announce before he returns with whatever he's found. I don't wait for him to reply. I'm focused on one thing and one thing only. I pull out my cell phone and find her social media account. She's not shared anything in a while. Most of her photos don't show her face. But I know every inch of her pretty pixie-like expression.

She's intelligent; I'll give her that. Hiding out comes easily to her. I'm sure with the years of practice, she's honed her skill, but she's not good enough to elude us.

Her photos hide most of what she looks like but still show off her alluring smile. It shines like a light. Each image may not be entirely focused on her face, but those with glimpses of her eyes show warmth in them.

It's what lures the ice-cold monsters closer.

Because bastards like us will watch, we'll prey, and then, we'll capture.

Three
LUCILLE

T HE MOON HANGS IN THE SKY LIKE A BEACON. I WANTED to run away, and I did. The big city wasn't for me. I had to leave because if I were anywhere close to the families my father destroyed, I would have, over time, lost my mind.

Nothing prepares you for the guilt that comes along with knowing you have the blood of a monster running through your veins. He was a monster. My father was evil. Which is why I find myself here, in a city on the other side of the world, away from anyone who would know me. But even so, someone might have followed the trial. They may have seen me in court. Life doesn't afford you anonymity when your father is a killer.

I didn't want to leave our home, but my mother

said it was for the best, which is why I'm living in London now where nobody knows my name. It will offer me the safety I want. My father is still behind bars. I wait every day for the news to come that he's escaped. He has too many connections with a lot of money. They have pull on law enforcement. I don't doubt he will break out. It hasn't yet, but who knows what will happen when it does.

I glance in the mirror to make sure my outfit is perfect. I started doing this because the loneliness has taken its toll. That's a lie. It's what I tell myself to appease the aching need as it continues to grow inside me.

I do this because there is darkness inside me.

Perhaps it's my father's influence, his broken parts have taken root in me, and now I'm slowly shattering. Tears fill my eyes, but I don't allow them to fall. It's almost time.

I make sure to darken my eyebrows and slip in the contacts which change the shade of my irises, and I'm no longer the offspring of a man who slaughtered so many.

I'm a stranger.

And I like it like that.

In my kitchen, I grab the bottle of wine and I pour a glass. The deep red sloshes against the sides before settling down. I pick it up and slowly sip the alcohol. A deep, spicy flavor bursts on my tongue.

It's almost nine, time to work.

Focus.

I cannot be intoxicated should anything happen.

Without another thought, I head into the second bedroom of my apartment and shut the door. It's the only way I can concentrate on what I'm about to do. I flick on the red light which illuminates the room in a deep glow.

The floor to ceiling windows offer a glimpse of a river snaking through the city. When I turn to my left, all I see are high-rise buildings, glinting with sparkling lights. To the right, I can about make out a few of the infamous sights of the city. It's turned cold over the past few weeks, and soon, I'll be able to take time off for Christmas.

A light flickers in a building opposite mine, but the rest of the windows are black, and I have to squint to figure out if I'm imagining things or if it's real. But it's gone within seconds, setting unease twisting in my gut. I imagined it. I must have. Maybe I'm thinking too deeply about things and it's someone coming home from work. But even as I consider this, I'm almost certain the building is only made up of offices.

I wait for another flicker, but it doesn't happen again.

My life has changed. Each time I notice an oddity— like flickering lights—I need a solid explanation, or my mind plays tricks on me. I turn away from the window and settle on the large mattress overlooking the camera.

The first time I did this, I felt ashamed afterward. But while I was online, I basked in the attention. One man at a time, where I can't see him, but he can see most of me. The parts men enjoy.

I've accepted my fate.

My future to live a life in solitary. When my father was arrested, I was put away with him. The confinement of my life has taken a toll, and now my needs have twisted into something far darker than I expected.

I flick on the camera, and log into my creator account. While I wait, I turn on the stereo, and music gently purrs through the speakers. The haunting voice of Digital Daggers sings "The Devil Within" while I sip my drink.

"Slut," a deep voice comes from the computer, and I know he's here. This is what I need, what I crave. I deserve nothing more than to be degraded because I'm broken.

"Yes, sir," I murmur, offering him a seductive and alluring smile. I found this website by chance, and since the first time I put on a show, I was addicted to the darkness these men enjoy.

"Spread those pretty legs for me," he orders, and I obey. "Mm," he groans, and I know he's turned on by the black lace covering my most intimate parts. He doesn't do anything more than order me around, asking me to touch myself, to explore my body, while calling me vulgar names.

I don't make a sound. Instead, I drop my hand between my thighs, and I tease my clit over the soft material. I'm wet. Drenched. A ding on the computer sounds, and my eyes snap to the screen. Furrowing my brow, I lean in closer, trying to see what it was.

"Is my slut misbehaving?" my client growls and I can practically feel his frustration. I'm not sure why, but ice trickles down my spine.

"No, I'm sorry," I tell him as I take my position again. But another ding sounds, and it's then I realize the cash amount. I've always been paid through a secure link, never in the chat rooms. But someone is in here, someone is watching, and I don't know who it is.

The amount continues to rise with every ding of the speakers. I drop my feet to the carpet and sit with my legs closed. I know this is going to lose me a client, but my gut churns with anxiety as I note there is now almost ten thousand dollars in my account.

"Slut," Mr. J spits with venom this time. "You're a useless fucking whore tonight," he tells me, as he clicks out of the room. The stranger is still here though because I see the guest icon blinking. He's watching, but he's turned off his speaker and camera. I can't see who it is, and the thought sets me on edge.

Then the text box pops up with a message making my blood run cold.

We're coming, little mouse. We're going to catch you and make you squeal.

My heart drops to my feet as I rush to the computer to shut it off. I'm kneeling on the floor, my heart thudding in my throat, choking me with every passing second. I didn't expect this night to go like this, but right now, fear has gripped me in its icy hold.

The last time I was so scared, was the night I learned who my father truly was. The other person in the chat room couldn't be connected. I try to convince myself of this, but I don't know for sure.

I want to escape. I need to run.

My fight or flight instincts kick into high gear, and I rush from the room into my personal bedroom and pull on a pair of sweats and an oversized hoodie. I can't be in here. I grab my keys and wallet along with my phone and race from the apartment. I step out onto the sidewalk and take a long deep breath.

I need to be around people.

Turning left, I make my way down to the pub. It sits on the corner, two streets from where I live, and inside, I find it warm and inviting. It's not overly busy, but there are a few regulars who are nursing their beers.

"What can I get you, love?"

"A double shot of whiskey, please?"

With a nod, I watch as the barman pours my drink and sets it on the bar. With the recognition of some of the people I've seen around before in the pub, I feel at ease. Settling into a chair, I sip the strong alcohol with a wince before picking up my phone.

I should call my mother. Or message her at least. We've hardly spoken since I left. She wanted me to have a new life, so I obeyed. I came here seeking fresh start. The memory of her telling me to go assaults me.

When the taxi pulls up to our block, I pay him and get out of the car. The rain hasn't let up, and by the time I walk inside, I'm drenched. My mother is on the sofa, her hand gripping a bottle of bourbon while her cigarette dangles between her lips.

She did her best.

But now it's no longer enough.

Sure, she has a job. She pays the rent. But there's nothing more for her to do for me. I'm an adult. I've finished my studies for the most part. Now all I need is the experience.

"He's never getting out," she mumbles, her voice husky as she stares at our flat screen. It's not big, but the illumination on her face is a bright blue in the darkness of our apartment.

"I saw the conviction," I tell her as I drop my purse on the table and shrug out of my coat. "Are you okay?" Even as I ask her, I know it's stupid because she can't be. I'm certainly not okay, and I don't expect my mother to be either.

She offers me a sad smile. "I'm sorry I couldn't do more for you." I'm not sure what she means, but I settle on the armchair, taking the remote control and flicking through the channels. But it's no use, they're all warning us to be careful of the dangerous monsters out on the streets.

Thankfully, even if my father could get out, he doesn't know where we are. He doesn't know we moved from the home which held all those painful memories. We're no longer living in the city where he tortured so many families. If he were to break out, he'd have to track us down. Then again, he has connections. Dangerous ones.

"Maybe we should leave, move to a new country," I announce, but the suggestion only earns me a dark laugh. It's as if she's given up on us. I watch my mother swig more amber liquid and swallow it down as if it were water. I've seen her broken before. But she dragged herself back up. Right now, I don't know how to make her see we will get through this.

"You should leave."

"What?" My mouth pops open in shock as I regard her.

She turns to me, her eyes blazing as she inhales a lungful of air. "You heard me," she tells me as if I'm a child and I need explanations done slowly. "Pack your things," she says. "And walk out. Leave the fucking country if you want to."

Surprise grips me as my mother pushes to her feet. She's wobbly at first, but then steadies herself. Her focus is on the bottle as she swallows back the last of the drink. I can't find words to respond as she moves past me and makes her way to the kitchen.

Our apartment isn't massive, it's a two bedroom with open kitchen and living room, but it's comfortable. It's home.

I can't imagine being anywhere else.

"I still have a few classes to finish."

"Do them and leave," she says. "It's for your own good. I can't let him find you again." Once she delivers her message, my mother walks into her bedroom, slams the door shut, and leaves me alone with nothing more than a broken heart.

It was then I knew I needed a new existence. A new identity. I needed to leave the country as she suggested. Which brings me to London, where the sky is always gray, and history seeps into my bones.

I didn't think I'd like it. I thought I would miss home, but I don't. I'm surprised by this because I'm not a lover of change.

But now I find myself somewhere new, with a chance at a normal life. If I can even call it that. I'm lonely because I don't know anyone, and dating is out of the question. I tried it, but each time I crave the darkness, I scare the men off. I beg for them to be rough, for them to hold me down, to choke me. The feel of fingers wrapping around the column of my neck is what I seek, and yet they're too fearful to do it. I want tears in my eyes as pleasure courses through me.

Only one person stuck through it, and even then, I sent him away in the middle of the night when he tried to ask me if I was okay.

I finish my drink and set the glass on the bar before waving a goodbye and stepping out into the chilly evening. The streets are still packed with people, and the bustle is a welcome distraction.

But as I make my way home, ice trickles down my spine, and it's not because of the weather. I glance behind me, casting a look over my shoulder as I try to see where the eerie feeling is coming from.

Turning to my front, I slam into a body so hard it reminds me of a slab of granite. My palms grip the material of the jacket which is soft to the touch. I tilt my head, and glance into the most hypnotic, yet piercing blue eyes I've ever seen.

"I'm sorry," I mumble, but the stranger doesn't say anything in return. He stares long and hard at me, as if he's trying to place my face from a memory. If he is, I pray it's not working. His mouth opens slightly but he doesn't say anything.

His jaw is smooth, angular as if it's been cast from marble. I can't tell what color his hair is because it looks buzzed, but it is dark. A hoodie covers his head, and I wonder briefly if I can push it down to get a better look.

His sharp features are made more prominent by his nose which is slightly crooked as if he's been in a fight and it healed off center. It makes him rugged, handsome but in a dangerous way. As if he can easily throw a punch without fear of the repercussions. Men like him are volatile. I should stay away.

The man looks like he should be on the front line carrying heavy weaponry, not on the city streets of London. But then again, I shouldn't be here either. I should still be living in a small town where everyone knew my name. The place cast me out because my father is a well-known monster.

"I'm sorry." I don't know why I'm repeating myself. He grunts. It's the only sound that comes out of him and he turns on his heel and stalks away. His broad shoulders, and long muscled legs make him seem even more dangerous as he leaves me staring at him.

It's a strange occurrence. One I don't want to repeat. Running into strangers isn't on my to do list, now, or ever. I move quickly up the road and watch as people pass me. Another man glances at me and for a second, I see *those* eyes. But when he turns away, I realize I'm hallucinating. It's not my father, it's only an innocent man who's trying to get home.

I wonder how in one short night my life can take on a whole new meaning.

It's happened before.

I have a feeling it's about to happen again. But I can't quite pinpoint how or why.

I think back to the stranger, how good it felt to be in somebody's arms again. I haven't been with a guy I craved before. At twenty-one, I should be out having fun. I should have friends who drag me to parties, but instead, I'm racing home to hide from the darkness outside, only to revel in the darkness on the inside.

Four
LUCILLE

MY ALARM SCREECHES IN THE DARKNESS OF THE ICY wintery morning, causing me to shoot up in bed. An eeriness hangs over the bedroom, and in the shadows of the space, it's as if I feel eyes on me. As if someone is watching. With a racing heart, I flick on the bedside lamp to find myself alone in my room.

There isn't anyone here, but I can't deny the past few days have been strange. Since the mysterious client logged into my chat room, and the stranger I bumped into on the street, I've been on edge.

I can't quite put my finger on it, but it feels as if I'm being followed everywhere I go. Pushing off the bed, I head into the bathroom, and catch a glimpse of myself in the mirror. I look exhausted. At least I have work today, which means I will be around people. The small coffee shop in the business district is constantly busy, allowing me to forget anything bothering me and focus on the rush.

I step into the shower before turning on the taps. The cold water is a shock to my system, but I'm awake, and shivering as the warmth slowly calms down my erratic pulse. Closing my eyes, I breathe in the steam as it billows around me, and soon I'm calm again. But as I lean against the tiles, lathering my skin, I think back to the stranger. His tall, broad body was so imposing, it was as if he could pick me up and sling me over his shoulder.

The thoughts turn darker, more sordid, as I imagine him stealing me from my life of hiding, and claiming me as his. Thick fingers tease my flesh, and a gruff growl of pleasure rumbles in his chest as my own fingers fall between my thighs.

Pleasure rockets through me at the contact. I'm needy, slick with arousal. I don't open my eyes. I can't. As wrong as it is to fantasize about a dangerous stranger, I don't stop because I need this.

I'm so close. Right on the edge when a crash startles me back to reality. Shutting off the taps, I step out on wobbly legs before wrapping myself in a towel. I wait in the bathroom, trying to listen for more sounds, but none come.

Barefoot, I pad into the bedroom, then make my way slowly to the kitchen, where I realize the window is open. My curtain sways in the wind. I find the broken glass in the sink, and for a moment, I sigh, but then I step closer to inspect the shards. Under the glass, placed neatly is an envelope.

My stomach churns with unease, and ice skitters down my spine. Gently shifting the glass, I pick up the thick white envelope which has my name scrawled on the front. I don't recognize the handwriting, but when I flip it over, I find a wax sealed crest. It looks like wings, but there's something sinister about them. They're not soft looking, as if feathers, but instead, blades.

I drop it on the counter, not wanting to touch whatever is in it. I don't know who put this here, but they must have been inside my apartment. The kitchen window is seven flights up with nothing on the other side. There is no balcony or landing for someone to stand on.

My gaze flicks across the room, the open plan living room kitchen area is empty, except for the furniture. There is no boogeyman standing and looking at me.

Silence hangs heavily over me. I can't waste time with this, or I'll be late for work. But I know I need to see what's inside. My curiosity wins out and I break the seal, which has dread coursing through my veins.

Inside is a simple card. Thick, expensive paper

in a cream color, with gold frame around the edges. Within the slim shimmering lines, is the same script as on the outside of the envelope.

Goldilocks,

Vengeance will be ours. The Fallen seek payment and you know why, little mouse. We're watching you. We'll come for you. When you least expect it, you will be ours.

The Fallen

I drop the card on the counter, shifting back until I hit the sink behind me. My vision blurs as I recall my father's transgressions. I always knew someone would find me. But I didn't think they'd be all the way over here, in another country. It seems my father's sins are mine to pay.

If I run, they'll find me. I have a feeling whoever these people are, they have the means to track me down no matter where I am. They've come all this way, which means one of the families my father destroyed needs revenge.

Sliding down against the cupboard, my butt hits the floor and I allow my tears to fall. It was stupid of me to think I could run from my past. I should have known no matter where I go, or what I do, my blood is still his. It runs through my veins, and now whoever this is has found me, they'll find out how much like my dad I am.

If I call Mom, she'll tell me to come home. But I can't. I need to face these people and beg for their forgiveness. I can't give up. I have to fight. It's not my sins they're angry for, it's the man who's behind bars. He's paying for what he did.

With newfound confidence and anger running through my veins, I push to my feet and focus on the day. I need to get to work. The sooner I'm around people, the less scared I'll be. I can't let the note get to me.

I get dressed quickly, leaving the broken glass in the sink. I shut the window, ensuring it's locked. Before I leave, I cast one last glance at the card on the counter, but I don't touch it. If I don't feel it in my fingers, perhaps it will disappear by the time I get home tonight. Deep down, I know I'm lying to myself.

Out on the road, I head for the bus stop. It's icy out today. There are already people rushing to work, to the gym, or making their way home from a late night out. I settle on the bench, waiting for the bus, when I can't stop a shiver racing through me.

Someone is watching me. I'm almost certain. Flicking my gaze around, it's difficult to tell with so many people around, but I get a distinct feeling I'm not alone. It sounds strange when I think about it, but it's there—I'm being watched.

I glimpse a dark figure across the road, down a small pathway which leads between two high rise buildings, but the moment I blink and open my eyes again, it's gone. Perhaps I'm losing my mind. Maybe I'm imagining people who aren't there.

The bus arrives, and I get on, but I'm still trying to spy if someone was standing there. As we pull out into the traffic, I look down the narrow road, and see it's empty. I really am going crazy.

Shaking my head, I pop my earbuds in and flick on a playlist, hoping it will distract me. The haunting voice of Echos sings through the small speakers. The familiar song, "Saints" plays as I make my way to work. But even music doesn't distract me and there's still a cold gripping me, holding me hostage.

By the time I walk into the coffee shop to start my shift, I'm only a few minutes late. Rushing behind the counter, I fall into the routine of taking orders, making the drinks, and serving the customers already standing in line.

"Hey girl," my colleague, Sarah, greets when we have a quiet moment. "You look tired," she tells me something I know.

Shrugging, I sip my own coffee, enjoying the heat of the java. "It's been a long morning already," I tell her, causing her to laugh out loud. "How are you?"

"I'm good. Maybe you should ask Darryl for

a few days off," she suggests, and for a moment, I ponder it. I can't really afford to take too much time off, but perhaps a few days might do me some good.

"Yeah," I say with a nod. "Maybe you're right." We get busy soon after, and we're not able to talk again as rush hour starts and we're lost to the number of orders coming through. I'm handing over a large latte when a deep, gruff voice skitters down my spine.

"Americano, no sugar," he says, and I glance up to find familiar blue eyes reminding me of an ocean. It's the stranger from the other day. I'm almost sure it's him. It was dark when I slammed into him, however those eyes are unmistakable.

"I know you," I whisper, shock so clear in my voice.

The corner of his mouth quirks infinitesimally, but I see it. The glower he pins me with after though has me practically shrinking away. "I doubt it." It's three more words which only confirms the husky gravel in his tone which has the hair on the back of my neck stand up.

"Luce," Sarah calls to me, distracting me from the handsome, dangerous looking man before me. "Orders up," she tells me and slides the large takeaway cup over to the man in question. He turns without another word and leaves the shop, and I'm still staring at the door, looking for him long after he's gone.

What are the odds of me bumping into the same person twice within days of each other? The city is big, it's busy, and I hardly ever see the same people I've crossed paths with which is exactly why I chose it. Making connections can be dangerous, and I can't put anyone else in danger.

The dark hoodie he wore reminded me of the figure I saw in the narrow road across the street from the bus stop. But it wouldn't make sense. *Why would he be watching me, or following me?*

Unless…

"Are you okay today?" Sarah asks when we settle into a quiet stint before lunch time. Her gaze is filled with worry, and I know I've not been myself.

"I have this feeling something bad is about to happen," I tell her, before looking at the door again. There are no customers lined up, nobody waiting to get into the store, but deep down, I wonder if *he* is out there watching from afar.

"Aw no, love," Sarah says as she grips my arm in an affectionate hold. "You need to take some time off. Maybe you need a spa weekend somewhere quiet. The city is clearly getting to you." I know she's trying to be nice, but frustration blooms in my gut. I don't want to be this person, living in fear. It's the reason I left the States. Knowing my father was so close by and he could find me at the drop of a hat caused me to constantly be on edge.

"I don't know if it's the city, or shit going on in my mind. I tend to have a vivid imagination," I tell her mostly the truth. Nobody knows me, the real me, and I like to keep it that way. Even if Sarah is a good friend, someone who I could probably talk to, I don't want her to see the broken parts of me.

"I stand by what I said," she tells me. "Ask for a few days off. Take a fortnight and head up to the Lake District." I've always wanted to go out there, it looks beautiful. Perhaps I can play tourist for a little while.

"I'll think about it," I tell her finally, and as busy as the rest of the day is, I'm still on edge. By the time I get home and see the note waiting for me where I left it this morning, I know whatever is coming won't be good.

Five
FALCON

ONCE I'M ALONE, I SCOUR THE INTERNET, THE DEEP dark fucking web. There are sites on here which would make the most violent killer squirm. I've seen it all before. My past is nothing more than a memory at this point, but each time I close my eyes, there's only blood I see.

Crow and Hawk have suffered as much as I have. We've banded together, like brothers, closer than any family I've ever known. While scrolling through the websites, my office door opens, and I glance up to see Hawk saunter in with a plate of food and the scent is like heaven and sex all rolled into one.

"Made you dinner," he says in his usual controlled, stoic tone.

"Thanks, man." It smells incredible. I don't ask where Crow is because I know he's probably hiding out in his bedroom. Since I first met him, I've come to learn he is a loner. He has us around, but he enjoys the quiet, which I understand. But there are times it gets too much. There are moments where I need companionship.

"Crow's stressed."

I look at one of my best friends and grin. "He's always fucking stressed," I tell Hawk as I stab the pasta with a fork and shove it into my mouth. "I'll find the psycho stalking her," I say as I click on the next website, scrolling for the name he used on the message board. But before I can, a ping sounds on my tracking app.

Hawk is on his feet. He knows the sound. He knows exactly what it means. "What's that?" He rounds the desk, stopping behind me as he leans in to look at the screen from over my shoulder.

When I open the page, I take note of the green dot flashing on the map. "She's on the move." The phone rings, and usually I'd enjoy the sound of the song alerting me to a call, but this time, I'm anxious. "What?"

"Do you think she's running?" he asks me. One of the only men I trust other than my Fallen brothers is Dante Savage. We met when I was working in the underground hacking community. We stumbled on each other's code, and when we came face to face, something clicked.

The guy is as fucking broken as we are, but when he told me his story, I felt sick to my stomach learning about what he and his brother Drake had been through. Since then, we've been in contact, and when he needs something, I'm happy to help and vice versa. It's good to keep connections, especially in the world we live in. He hasn't steered me wrong yet.

"She's not heading into work. And we know she doesn't have friends she hangs out with. We need to know where she's going. Follow her," I tell him. "I'm tracking her cell phone, but I haven't noticed anything out of the ordinary all morning." With my focus on the call log, I click onto the refreshed page and my chest tightens. There has been one number calling incessantly for the past hour. It didn't refresh because I've been working on something else. Now I'm staring at the screen, my gut churns.

"You see it. Don't you?" Dante asks, and I nod to myself.

I throw out the only word which expresses how I feel. "Fuck."

"Yeah. I'm on it." He hangs up before I can respond.

"We need Crow—"

"What the fuck is going on?" The man in

question stalks into the office, his face a picture of anger and frustration. I don't blame him. I'm also fucking rage-filled. I should have anticipated she's clever.

"She's running, or something. She's been getting calls from a number with an American code for the past hour. The call log shows it rings every minute."

"I don't like this," Crow grits through clenched teeth. His jaw ticks, his hands fist at their sides when he nears the desk. "We need to get out there."

"I have Dante on her tail," I inform him. "Hawk can get to her before she does something stupid." It's a plan which eases the tension in Crow's shoulders as they visibly relax.

"Do it."

Hawk is out the door before we can say anything more. This is something he enjoys. The chase. Being a retired soldier has given him the instincts of a killer, and his stint in MMA has allowed him the strength to take down any bastard who tries to get in his way.

Crow paces the carpet in front of my desk, and I wish he would leave me to my work. The app beeps with Hawk's location, and I map out Lucille's location for him. It will link up to his phone, ensuring he'll be able to find her quickly. We weren't going to bring her here for at least another week, but it looks like our little Goldilocks will be our guest sooner rather than later. She went underground when her father was arrested, and it was my job to keep tabs on her, and her mother. Since the mom is still Stateside, there hasn't been much movement.

But Lucille has been working in London for almost a year now. When we moved over here to settle, I knew Crow chose the smallest town close to London so we could get to her if needed.

The house that sits in a quiet little town is our home. It's old gothic architecture lends to the eeriness of the location. A cemetery flanks the grounds to the rear, and the hills of green farmland offer views from the front door.

It's stunning. A picture postcard.

But what happens inside the walls of our home, is another story. Since three monsters live here, and soon we'll have a pretty little golden princess to taunt until she gives up the location of her father's associates.

He wasn't working alone. We know that much. Now he's trying to contact her, because there is no other person who would call her from home. Her mother is still in a home, being looked after, so the number which has been ringing her must be him or one of his cronies.

When you have connections in every law enforcement agency in the world, and the money to buy the information you need, you learn a lot. It's why we're so good at our jobs.

"Do you need something to do?" I quip teasingly, glancing at Crow.

"Don't give me shit for being anxious," he throws back, and I can tell he's craving blood. There's a dark, sordid part of Crow none of us have truly seen yet. He doesn't kill innocent people, but he enjoys slaughtering bastards who deserve it.

We settle into silence with Crow walking back and forth in front of me, while I continue my search on who is looking for our girl. She's ours. There's no doubt about it, and when we get her here, at least we'll know she's safe.

As safe as she can be living in a house with three violent psychopaths.

"Fuck," I curse when I finally find something. Crow is beside me in seconds. The anxiety he's emitting is like a goddamned cologne. "Would you calm the fuck down?"

"No. Not until she's under our roof." I can't argue. "What did you find?"

"Her father has been making inquiries. His connections on the outside are tracking our girl." We should have seen this happening, but we didn't. I didn't. When it comes to tracking and hacking, I'm the fucking king, but I missed it. I know it could have our plan teetering on the edge of falling apart.

"Who are these bastards?" Crow's voice has turned to hunger. "I'll find them."

When my code throws back an address, Crow is out the door before I can say anything. I watch him race from my office and I can't help but smile. There are sights I can never tire of and looking at Crow from any angle is one of those.

When I first met him, he was fighting with one of the boys at school. A bully. The asshole had stolen some girl's lunch, and Crow had taken it upon himself to play the hero. Over the years, after the heartache his family had suffered, he's changed. He isn't a hero anymore, but there is still a goodness inside him. Something I have loved about him since the moment I saw it.

He's loyal to a fault. He will kill for those who he cares for, and he has, so many times before. Once for me. I owe him my life because of it. Sitting back, I watch the map as it tracks both Hawk and Crow, as well as our little Goldilocks.

She'll soon be here, and when she is, it will be like we planned. Hawk reaches her on the map, the two dots inches from each other, and I smile. Soon, he'll have her in his car, leaving the piece of shit she drives at the side of the road. We'll have Dante sort it out, but for now, the focus is on getting her here before anyone else finds her. Crow on the other hand is making his way to our stalker's house, which will be another hour.

My phone rings on the desk, the vibration the

only sound in the room. Picking it up, I glance at the screen to the unknown number staring back at me. Usually, I don't answer calls like this, they're all screened, but I'm anxious to know if the bastard who was watching Lucy has noticed I hacked into his systems.

"Yes?"

"I need your services," a deep voice comes from the other end of the line. "It has to be done within the next week."

A grin curls my lips. "We don't run on client's time. Our jobs are completed on our time." Whoever this is, doesn't realize we're not slaves, and we're not cheap guns for hire who can be ordered around.

We run the jobs.

Not them.

"Fine." He sounds frustrated, but I don't give a shit. "Then, I need your help with a time sensitive job."

"It's not a problem," I tell him easily. "You'll email information through to me and we will get on it as soon as we can. The deposit is paid within an hour of your details being received, and the rest of the payment is due once we locate the person it is you're looking for."

"And you're able to do *anything* I want?" The way he questions, the way he voices the word *anything* sets me on edge. My hackles rise at the thought of what this fucker wants from us.

"As long as you're willing to pay the price," I tell him easily, but he must know we have rules. There is a list of items which would hinder our services moot. Even if he's paid, if we deem it morally wrong, we don't complete a job. It makes me chuckle under my breath when I think about how morally wrong kidnapping a pretty blonde girl is. Yet, here we are, poised to steal Lucy and bring her into our den.

"I have more money than God," the man on the phone tells me. "I can pay anything you want," he says confidently.

The corner of my mouth tilts with satisfaction. If he were to request something we won't do, he'll be the one to pay with something far more expensive than his life. It will be his heart on a fucking platter.

"You'll receive a text message at the number you're calling from. An email address will be sent to you in the next few minutes. We need all the information of the job in question, once you've sent it through, the banking details will be confirmed."

"What do you—"

"I'm the professional in this equation, Mr. Simmonds," I interrupt him with a smile on my face. "Don't underestimate our reach, or our power," I inform him coolly. It only took me a few minutes to trace the number, location, and name of the man on the other end of the line. "Because I can dig through records to find out everything about you. Now, I trust all is in order."

"Y-y-yes," he stutters before I hang up and send the text message. I don't doubt he'll be corresponding with us soon about whatever it is he needs. With a quick look at his social media accounts, I can already deduce we won't like him. A family man with a fake smile and lies in his gaze.

I don't want to think about what it is he needs from us. Another beep alerts me, telling me there's movement. I've been ignoring the map while on the call. Hawk is in place. The small green dot confirms our little doll is heading out to parking lot which doesn't make sense. She's in public, which is the only thing keeping him from stealing her.

I wonder if she can feel the end is coming. If she can sense our presence. While I think about her nighttime chats with a stranger on the internet, I can't help my dick getting hard. When I first found her, I thought she was like any other straight A student. But she's got a darkness residing inside her. Perhaps her father's influence isn't too far behind.

Goldilocks logs into her computer every night at nine. While she's alone, she chats to strangers, getting her pretty pussy off to the filthy things men tell her. I can't deny I've jerked off to her countless times.

Crow walked in on me the first time and he

gave me an earful, but when I showed him her preferences, he realized she may not be the pristine little doll we thought she was. No, this girl likes it rough. She enjoys humiliation and degradation.

I've looked into her past, and I am certain it comes from the trauma she suffered as a young girl. Watching your father kill innocent kids must have fucked with her mind. Hawk reckons it's her *escape,* but I think there's something more to it.

I have a feeling she enjoys the darkness, but she's too afraid to play in it for real.

The moment she's in our home, under our roof, I'm going to test my theory. And when I do, I'm going to listen to the pretty little toy sing for me. I'm going to make her scream, cry, and come, all over my fingers and tongue, and when she's spent, I'm going to see how well she takes my cock.

My attention is caught by the map flickering with Crow's location. He's arrived at the house. He won't be long. In, kill, out. When he gets home, all three of us will have our brand new toy, and I can't wait to play.

Six
HAWK

*P*RETTY LITTLE GIRL.
My thoughts deter me from focusing on the road which is not a good idea. I head out to watch her every night. Falcon keeps watch on me, tracking me. Sometimes, I turn my phone off so he doesn't know how long I spend outside her apartment.

At other times, I allow him to see through my eyes.

I've become accustomed to standing guard, waiting for the moment I'm ready to snatch her up. She's ours. She has been for a long time. We waited until she didn't have obligations. Her schooling is complete, and she's old enough for us to capture and do with as we wish. It's the perfect time to take her away.

When the map steers me back toward her place, I hit dial on Falcon's number to ensure it's not sending me the wrong way.

"She's backtracking," Falcon answers with a response to my unasked question. "Not sure why, but keep on her tail. You should see Cypher as well."

"I don't need backup," I grunt in frustration. As much as I know Cypher helps with his underground connections, I don't like the bastard. I don't like anyone for that matter. Except for my brothers, they're the only people I do trust. The only men I'll ever kill for.

"Stop being a grumpy bastard."

"Not my fault nobody can be trusted," I throw back as I sit back and enjoy the ride. I can see her car in front of me. I've left two spaces between us, which means she won't notice I'm right behind her until it's too late.

Falcon sighs on the other end of the line, as he always does when I'm in a bad mood. "Fine. I'll call him off, but don't get lost inside your head." He knows I tend to lose myself in memories. But with Lucy to watch, I don't think I'll find it too difficult to focus.

"I know how to do my job," I inform him. When she takes a left toward her apartment block, I realize she's going home. Which makes me wonder why she left in the first place. I pull into a parking spot when she steps up to the building. "She's at the apartment," I tell him.

"I wonder what made her run." Falcon voices my thoughts exactly.

"Call Cypher off, and I'll see you later," I tell him and hang up before he can say anything more. There's no need to continue a conversation, it will lead nowhere. I keep my gaze on the building before me. The moment the lights in her apartment flicker on, I sit back and wait.

It's winter, which means it won't be long before the sun is gone. I prefer working at night. The darkness allows me to move without being noticed. The little blonde moves around her apartment, and I'm thankful for the windows offering a glimpse into her life.

She's alone, and in the dark, I can't deny my craving for her is at an all-time high. I never thought a woman could make me feel like this, but Lucille does. Since we started watching her, I've become more than obsessed. The guys know it's in my nature. My focus homes in, and I can't stop my mind from running through scenarios, learning and researching our targets. But I think there's something dark inside her and it calls to my own demons.

We've bumped into each other a few times. She can feel someone watching her, but she doesn't know which shadow is real, and which is in her imagination. We've toyed with her, but it's time to bring our Goldilocks home. The nickname came to me the first time I saw her.

But as beautiful as she is, as hard as she makes my cock, her father still ruined my life. Torturing her will be fun. Hearing her screams will only ensure my need for her grows, but I have no problem with the increasing desire for her, because I plan to have her. I want to taste every inch of her silky smooth flesh.

My phone vibrates in my pocket, but I don't look at it. I know it's Falcon. He can see I'm not moving. The tracking will show him I'm observing. I have to because kidnapping a woman isn't easy. Not when there are outside factors which could play into this.

One thing I learned over the years is you can't take chances. It's the difference between life and death. She moves through her apartment, unaware of my eyes on her. My jeans are tight at the crotch as I watch her change.

A groan rumbles in my chest when I take in the beauty. Too bad she's going to hurt so badly, she'll beg us for death. It doesn't matter what she says though, she has to pay. Her father may be locked away, and we can't get to him, but there are ways to ensure he learns his actions have consequences.

She slips into her loose-fitting hoodie over a tank top, doing nothing to hide her curves. Her long hair shimmers in the low light of her bedroom as she pulls it into a ponytail and my fingers itch to wrap those long strands around my fist.

What I wouldn't do to have her bent over in front of me right now. Shifting in my seat, I lay a hand on my hard cock to ease the ache of my slowly thickening shaft. I bet she's tight and warm. I can't stop imagining her slick walls pulsing around me.

Fuck. I need to get out of this car. I shove open the door then step out into the cold night air and it hits me right in the face. It's as if icicles are being thrown at me. Thankfully, it calms my raging hard on and I can focus once more.

Once her light goes out, I know it's time to make my move. I open the trunk of my car, then pull out the rope and grab the cloth which I'll douse once I'm outside her door. She won't feel a thing, and it will keep her quiet while I drive home.

Moving through the shadows, I focus on the task at hand as I make my way into the building. It's not manned by security, which is lucky, but also a shame for our girl. I thought she'd be more vigilante about where she lives. Perhaps she thinks being in another country has kept her safe from her father and his actions.

When the elevator spits me out on her floor, I step out into the quiet hallway and turn left. Outside her door, I open the small bottle of chloroform. Once

I've soaked the cloth, I move quickly, picking the lock of her apartment and stepping inside.

The scent of her perfume lingers in the air, and I realize our home is about to be drenched in her fragrance. A smile plays at my lips, but I shut it down and move through the darkness until I reach her bedroom.

For a while, I lean against the door jamb, watching her. She's not asleep yet, so I wait. I don't have anywhere to go, there's no rush. Her body is tangled in the sheet, her long, lean legs in view. The smooth skin is a soft golden shade of tanned perfection.

Silence hangs in the air heavily, ensuring I'm not heard as I breathe deeply. She truly is beautiful. The honeyed perfume she wears is dangerous because my mouth waters at the thought of pinning her on the bed and taking what I want, devouring her with my mouth as I trail over the softness of her curves.

It's been a long while since I've looked at a woman with any ounce of desire. Lust yes, where I'm able to get my dick wet, but nothing more. I don't spend the night. Most women learn about my needs, and they run a mile. I am not conventional in any sense of the word. I don't do sweet, romantic, and loving.

Perhaps it's the past constantly plaguing me and pushing me into the darkness. Maybe it's the fact I love watching a woman beg for mercy. When her body is overstimulated, and she's lost in euphoria, there's an edge of agonizing want holding her hostage. When she's come so much it hurts, the destructive line I teeter on, wanting her to beg for mercy, burns me from the inside out. It's enjoyable watching her legs shake and her back bow off the bed. Knowing you're the one in control of her every emotion, her every movement, it's intoxicating.

Ideas pop into my head, things we could do to her. Picturing her at the hands of my brothers, I can't deny it turns me on more than I could have imagined. Knowing how much Crow loves to play with knives, and how Falcon enjoys rope and toys, and how I'd love nothing more than to taste their salty release on her skin, sends me reeling.

With a fierce grip on the door frame, I dig my fingers in. My mind isn't a nice place to be. It's why I fight. I enjoy the ring where I can bloody up someone without consequences. I don't give a shit about being thrown in the slammer. As The Fallen, we have the money and connections to cover up anything. But there's a brutality in the ring which doesn't happen in the streets.

When my phone vibrates again, I know I'm going to have to make a move. Either I take her now or listen to Crow complain about delaying the plan. I don't want to hear him lose his cool about this. The sooner we have her in our home, the quicker we can get the information we need, and make sure her father knows exactly what we did.

A smile graces my lips. It's dark, nobody can see it. The guys consider me the serious one, but there are many things which bring me pleasure. This time, it's the thought of the cameras in Lucy's bedroom at home are something I'm going to revel in.

I can sit in the darkness and watch her. Something tells me this girl isn't going to be easy to break. I know from listening to Falcon's recollections she's into some kink shit. I wonder how she'll enjoy the three of us.

Making sure the cloth I have is soaked enough to knock her out, I make my move. My silent footsteps carry me right to her bedside where I stop for a moment. She is beautiful, too bad Crow will never allow her to survive this. If I had to be honest, neither would I. Watching her father's evil acts has ensured nothing this girl does will save her life.

I lean in, running my knuckles over her cheek gently. She doesn't stir, and I can't help but smile. So comfortable, so at peace, she doesn't realize the monster is right beside her. I press the cloth over her mouth and nose, pushing down hard.

Her eyes snap open, wide with shock, and her flailing arms try to attack me while her legs kick out, but she's weaker than I am. My strength overpowers her easily, and when she slowly loses her fight, I chuckle. I can only imagine the number of curse words she's spewing at me.

Her lashes flutter like a pretty butterfly's wings.

Once she stops moving, I lift her delicate frame into my arms, and I make my way out of her home. She won't see this place again. I take the back exit which offers me the cover I need. Once outside, I round the building and slink into the shadows with Lucille in my arms. Soon we're at the trunk where she'll sleep for the next hour on the drive to the house.

I should really put her in the backseat. I stare down at her body before I make my decision. Even if she does wake up, I'll handle her whining. Grabbing a ball gag from my little bag of tricks, I bind it around her head. The small black ball fits neatly between her plump lips.

The sight of her makes me hard as fuck. I put her in the backseat instead before I grab the rope, and bind her hands and ankles. I can't help smiling because I can only imagine how beautiful she would look in leather cuffs, pleading for her mercy as I snake a whip against her soft flesh.

Once I'm in the driver's seat, I tap out a message to let Falcon know I'm heading back. He'll see it on the map anyway. Putting the car into drive, I make my way home with my little captive who's sleeping soundly. It won't last long because the moment she wakes up, there will be hellfire coming from her mouth. And I'm thankful for the gag.

Time to play, Goldilocks…

Seven

LUCILLE

*T*HUD. *THUD. THUD.*

A throb of agony shoots through my head when I try to open my eyes. A groan vibrates in my chest as I shift on the hard surface beneath me, and more pain zaps down my left side when I roll over.

I manage to open one eye, when all I see is darkness. Both snap wide open, and my head shifts to try to figure out where I am, but there's complete black in front of me. My hands are bound behind me, and my arms scream as I attempt to tug at my restraints.

Nothing works.

My memories are fuzzy. Last night, I remember being home. I was in bed, having an early night, when I heard a noise. I'm pretty sure of it. The migraine holding me hostage has me wincing when I manage to swing my legs over the edge of whatever I'm lying on. Finally seated, I try to stand, but my legs are wobbly, sending me crashing back down onto the threadbare mattress.

Suddenly, bright light illuminates the space, blinding me momentarily.

"She's awake," a voice comes from somewhere int he room, but I can't open my eyes. The stark white of the bulb forcing me to keep my lids shut.

"Who are you? What's going on? Why am I here?" My voice croaks, my throat tight with fear as a lump forms, threatening to choke me to death. Perhaps it would be welcome, an escape from whatever the hell I've gotten myself into.

"She's prettier up close," another deep rumble says as the shuffle of heavy boots against cold concrete sounds in the room.

My spine tingles with awareness. They don't come closer. I can't hear any footsteps which means they're still at the entrance to the room which is still in pitch blackness. I'm certain there are three men, but the third hasn't spoken yet. He must be watching though.

A memory slams into me suddenly, and realization dawns on me. "You took me," I whisper. "You fucking kidnapped me you psychopaths!" I don't know why I'm taunting them, but I can't keep my mouth shut. Anger surges through me, overtaking the fear.

It's momentarily stunted by a harsh swat against my cheek which sends me reeling to the ground. I slam down onto the cold, hard concrete, my knees protesting as pain shoots up my legs.

"Shit," I bite out, cursing silently as I try to keep my mouth shut. If I were to say anything more, they'll surely kill me. I don't know what they want from me, but I kneel, my head bowed, and I don't move for a long while.

"I like you on your knees," the first man who spoke says. His voice is closer now, but I didn't hear him take any steps. Fingers tangle in my hair, twisting my head until I'm once again blinded by light. This time though, the illumination aids me, showing me the shadows who watch over me.

Three faces. They don't look human, but I know they are. They have to be. The skulls painted on their expressions are hard, cold, and deadly. If I were drunk, I may have thought I'd been killed and sent to hell.

But this is very much real.

At least, I think it is.

"What do you want from me?" My voice croaks on the last word, and tears sting my eyes. As much as I want to fight them, to tear their eyes from their heads, I can't move. I hate being weak.

"We're here to play a little game, Goldilocks," the one gripping my hair sneers. I want to respond, but I don't have time because he continues, "It's time we tell our story."

I vowed a long time ago I'll never again be weakened by a man.

Yet, here I am, on my knees, bound, at their mercy.

But something tells me they don't know what that word means.

"W-W-What do you mean?" I stutter, fear enveloping me. There is an icy chill in the room, basement, wherever I am. The men don't answer me, they merely take me in. One of them tilts his head to the side, the corner of his mouth lifting slightly making the fake *teeth* painted onto his face seem almost sinister.

I've witnessed people dressing up for Halloween with make up like this. I've seen it posted all over social media. It was a fad and it hasn't died out, and here they are, looking like they're ready for the party.

"Lucille," the tallest one says, as he flicks on a dim bulb hanging in the middle of the room. "I think it's time you formally met us." The weak illumination does nothing to ease my anxiety as the yellow glow shimmers over their faces. The hoods they wear cover their hair, so I can't tell much more than height and build.

What does startle me though is their eyes. The one in front who spoke first, who I'm guessing is the leader, has the most iridescent silver eyes. Like shining metal which seems to change into a variety of shades when he moves.

The other man to the leader's left is a head shorter, but he's broader. HIs wide shoulders fill out the black hoodie he's wearing, and his eyes are a deep aquamarine, a blue so light, so *clean*, it looks like a gemstone. Lastly, is the slender one with his hands in his pockets. He's smirking at me with amusement now, and his gaze of jade green is locked on me.

"You've been a bad, bad girl," *green eyes* says to me, his tone playful, but there's a hint of madness to it. As if he can flick a switch and his smiles can turn into sneers.

"I-I don't understand," I croak out, integrally berating myself for being so submissive. Granted, I'm afraid of them, of what they can do to me, but I don't want to appear weak. There is no way I can fight them off, but I won't go down without trying.

Silver eyes moves to the corner of the room, and it's only then I realize there's a chair. He settles himself into it, his legs spread wide, and it should be illegal for someone so sinister to look so good.

The darkness inside me craves the monsters, and it dances with delight. I've fought my demons, kept them at bay. It's only at night I allowed myself to delve into that side of my psyche. But here, with these dangerous men, I can't let it happen. I have to focus. I have to find a way to escape.

"We have a job for you," he informs me as he leans back in the chair, causing the wood to creak under his weight. He must be at least six-foot tall.

"I have a job," I tell him, finding my voice, praying they'll let me go. "And usually when I'm offered a job, I'm not kidnapped first."

"I heard you're the perfect one for this particular work though," he says slowly. There's something about him, he has a predatory aura which makes me shiver. This man doesn't do things out of haste, he plans, he's methodical. There is a reason I'm here. It's not by chance.

He wants me here.

They want me here.

"I didn't think you'd come otherwise," he informs me. "Also, we're not known in our circles as the most polite." This has the other man with his jade green eyes chuckling. I'm intrigued by the other one, he's been silent all this time.

I muster up my courage, and turn my attention to *silver eyes,* before I ask, "Tell me what this job is then? What is so important you couldn't find someone else to do it?"

"Before I go into the specifics, I want to see if you'll obey," he says, then, he leans forward, his elbows landing on his thighs and his fingers twining together. He gestures with his chin toward the other two before he commands, "Untie her."

It's the silent one who moves swiftly. He's quick with his hands and soon enough, I'm freed from my bindings. But I still can't move because even if I tried to run, they'd catch me before I made it to the door.

"You can try," *Silver eyes* murmurs. Something about his tone tells me he *wants* me to. He'll enjoy the chase, and I'll become a feast for the three of them to devour. I will not give them the satisfaction. "How about you drop to your knees for me?"

I snap my gaze to his, silver meeting gold. Metal against metal, I want to be stronger, I don't want to flinch at his glare, but I can't help it. "What?"

This time, he smiles and my inner demon dances once more. He's breathtaking. I can't describe him in any other way. Danger emanates off him like a cologne, it's intoxicating. All three of them are alluring, and the more I think it, the more I inwardly debate if I'm finally losing my mind.

"You heard me," he says before waving his hand. "Get on your knees." He straightens his back and reaches behind him. When his hand appears, he's holding a glinting blade. It looks like it could easily carve my skin from my bones. I don't have to touch it to know it's sharp. He meets my stare before saying, "I don't like waiting."

I have no choice. I obey the bastard as hatred burns through my veins. The fury I'm currently holding onto will give me the strength I need to kill this fucker the moment I find a way to.

He tuts, shaking his head as if I've disappointed him. I've done what he asked of me, but he seems to be upset about it. But then he explains, "You show your emotion on your face, Goldilocks."

The name makes me quirk my head. It seems I'm stuck in a house with the three fucking bears. Only, they won't allow me to live, it's the only thing I know for certain.

"Crawl to me." His order comes swiftly, and when I don't move quickly enough for his liking, he nudges his head and one of his friends nudges my butt with his shoe.

"Fuck you!" Even as I say it, I know it's a mistake because fingers tangle in my hair, and the sting of pain from my scalp makes my eyes water.

"Say it again, little girl," the hiss is from *green eyes*, the tone of his voice laced with amusement. I can picture him smiling as his lips brush along my earlobe causing me to shiver. "Please, say it again so I can show you what happens to disobedient pets."

My chest tightens and anxiety twists in my gut, reminding me I'm in danger. This isn't a game. This isn't an online chat room where I enjoy clients hurting me with their words.

"Or is that something you like?" His question has goosebumps rising on every inch of my body. He doesn't let up his hold on my hair. He seems to twist the long strands until I whimper. "Mm," he moans in my ear, the sound vibrating over my cheek. "That's the sound I want to hear," he informs me. "If you're a good girl, maybe I will hurt you and make you come all over my fingers."

"Falcon, enough." The order is swift, and pinched, then suddenly, I'm released from my prison and I fall onto my hands. I'm knelt before *Silver eyes* like a dog on all fours now. At least I know one of their names—Falcon. "Come to me," *Silver eyes* commands as he crooks his finger and I move.

I'm no longer fighting them because it won't get me out of this dungeon, I'm not sure what can. But I will obey until I figure it out.

"You're much prettier on the floor," he tells me. "I think you'll do well cleaning our home." He leans forward, before gripping my neck much as Falcon did, but before he says anything more, he shoves his fingers down my throat, and continues the motion as if he were fucking me with his cock.

Soft sounds of my gagging echoes in the room. The man before me smiles. He's enjoying this. Once last push of two digits, and I convulse, the bile rising up quickly, and before I have time to push him away, puke spills from my lips.

"Filthy little slut," he tells me as he regards his now dirty fingers while twisting them before those silver eyes. "You'll clean up, and our whole house will be spotless when you're done."

"You want me to be a maid?" My incredulous tone causes him to arch a brow. "I'm asking because I'm not sure why you'd think—"

"You will work for us, be our everything." He waves his hand in the air as if it explains it all. I'm more confused than ever. He can't mean I will have to sleep with them, I refuse to has sex with men like this. *Men like my father*. The thought attacks me violently as tears sting my eyes. "Anything we ask of you, you'll do."

I meet his stare, I don't blink, and I ask, "And why would I do that?"

For a long while, he looks at me, his gaze tracking over my body. I'm still in my pajamas and I realize then how cold I am. But after a long silence, he smirks with pure unadulterated satisfaction, and says, "Because it's time to pay for your father's sins."

Eight
CROW

THE SURPRISE ON HER FACE IS ENOUGH TO SATISFY ME FOR the evening. I push to my feet, causing her to fall back onto the floor. Her ass hits the cold concrete as I pass by. I'm not sure she won't attempt to run, so I decide we'll leave her here for the night.

"Let's go," I order the other two. Falcon was enjoying himself earlier, and I can't deny, watching them together made my dick hard. He knew what he was doing as well. Falcon likes to taunt and tease. I would love to see her coming all over his fingers. I would love to see her sweet, angelic face contort with pleasure.

"Wait," she calls to me, and I cast her a glance from over my shoulder. "Y-you know my father?" Her question has my blood turning hot with rage.

85

I want nothing more than to show her exactly what her father did, but it will come. It will be the first lesson she learns when we allow her upstairs.

"We knew him," Falcon answers for me because I can't bring myself to even talk about him to her. Not yet. I will though. There is a time and place for everything. My little mouse will learn. She's got so much light in her, it hurts to look directly at her, it's like looking into the goddamned sun. "Get some sleep."

Falcon is far too nice to her. I turn and glare at him before I make my way up the stairs. We need to talk about the house I found. It's no doubt her father's connections. I found things in there which will have the cops crawling all over it soon. I've seen some shit in my life when it comes to the bastard, but I'm always sickened by his acts. His acquaintances are no better. Whoever lived there was a vile fucker, and I wish I found him. I would love to introduce him to Indie, my blade.

By the time I reach the ground floor, I make my way straight to Falcon's cave. The office is a mess, but I shove paperwork to the side and flop onto the sofa. I'm tired. Drained from the recent events. Hawk settles in beside me and Falcon takes the seat at his desk.

"We have a new job," he says as he pushes papers around on the surface. I don't know how the hell he finds anything in the heap, but I don't say anything about it. My mind is still on her. The sweet scent of her fucking perfume is stuck in my nose. The sight of her on her knees before me had images dancing around in my head which I have no right to think. I shouldn't *want* her. She's here to repay her father's sins, like I told her.

But I can't deny she's stunning.

"Are you even listening to me?" Falcon's question breaks me of my reverie, and I pin him with a glare.

"What?"

"Jesus, two minutes with her and you're already falling in love?" His taunt is followed by a chuckle, and I move so swiftly, he about misses Indie shooting past his head landing in the expensive oak of his bookshelf behind his desk. "Hey!"

"Shut the fuck up about her," I bite out, frustration burning in my veins. My brothers know I don't do women. I don't date, I don't really fuck around. There are times I need a wet pussy, and I find it at the local pub, but usually, I don't go back for seconds.

Emotions destroy you, so I shut mine off a long time ago.

Falcon shakes his head, before continuing, "As I was saying. We have a new job. Some asshole who didn't know how powerful we are. He was trying to stall on the information when I found out his whole life history." This makes Falcon laugh. The bastard is a brilliant hacker.

"Did you get Cypher on the trail?"

"He's helping with tracking down all known associates of Mahoney," he informs me. It's been a long time since I heard his name. Lucille's father is a topic we don't go into detail about, but now she's here, we're going to have to face our past. Thing about it is, each time I've gone there in my mind, violence was the only way to ease me back to reality.

"What about the girl?" Hawk asks. It's the first time he spoke since I arrived back from the job to find out who was trailing Lucille.

"She's working for us now," I inform them both, and the questioning gazes I receive in response is enough to have me sighing. "She'll look after the manor. We can't do it when we're working, and I figured while she's here, she can offer her services." This makes me look over at Falcon. He's the one who found out about her extra-curricular activities. If she wants bad men to make her come, we can do it easily.

"Are you serious?" Falcon's shock is mirrored on Hawk's face. They weren't expecting it. I wasn't thinking about it until I saw her on her knees. I wouldn't mind getting a taste of the little slut. I bet her cunt is sweet as candy apples.

"I am." Pushing to my feet, I make my way to the patio doors and push them open. It's dark out, the chilly night air causes my breath to billow in white puffs. "She's here, she'll learn about vengeance the hard way. If she doesn't complete a task to our liking, she'll receive a punishment."

"But doesn't it make us as bad as—"

"Don't you fucking go there, Falcon," I bite out, grinding my teeth so hard, it's a wonder they're not broken. "She's an adult," I tell him. It's what I keep reminding myself. We waited until she was of age to take her. As much as I hate her father, I don't want to turn into him.

"What if she enjoys her punishments?" Falcon chuckles behind me.

"I don't doubt she will," I tell him before turning to both men. "When she experiences even an ounce of pleasure, we break her down. Each day, she'll become more and more submissive. I want to watch her shatter," I say as the thought of her on her knees, begging me to make her come assaults my mind with clarity. "The pain we bring to her will be brutal, none of the shit she plays with online."

"What about the twins?" I knew Hawk would ask about them. His parents had twins in the aftermath of what had happened all those years ago. His mother was pregnant, and now the boys are seven, they're going to come to England to attend school here. They will live with us when they're on their holidays, but other than that, the boarding school will be their home."

"She can babysit them," I tell him. "It's what she's good at." I pull out a smoke and light it, pulling in the nicotine deep into my lungs. I can't imagine having her around the boys. I've met them a few times when they've come to visit, and they're intelligent and curious like my brothers were.

"I can have them stay—"

"You know they're welcome here any time. They're family," I inform him. He nods when I glance over my shoulder. That's the end of the conversation. We will have Lucille live here, work for us, and become our toy. She'll take everything we give her, and I have a feeling she's not going to take it without a fight. I look forward to it.

"I think she's going to kick up a fuss down there," Falcon remarks with a sly grin I notice when I turn to face the room again. "I bet she's going to try to claw her way out." There is a small window which sits high in the wall. When the sun rises, she'll see it. But it's too small and too high for her to reach.

"I want the cameras on the room all night," I inform Falcon. "Call Cypher, let's hear what he's got." I settle back on the sofa beside Hawk who's silently resting against the leather back. He is a man of few words, and I wonder how he handled being so close to Lucille. I wanted him to be the one to grab her because I need him to come out of his shell, but something tells me I have a lot of work ahead of me.

"Twice in one week," Cypher greets over the call, catching my attention. "What can I do for you Falcon?"

"I need any intel you have," Falcon responds as he leans back in his enormous leather chair.

"Seems our man is connected to an underground trafficking ring which is still going even though he's behind bars. It's being run out of China, with links to Russia, and Colombia."

"Triad, Bratva, and Cartel?" I question in surprise. I wasn't expecting the combination of organizations. I knew Lucille's father was into some bad shit—he lost his mind and went on a killing spree—and now he's locked up, he's being kept safe in the penitentiary because they were afraid of what the inmates would do to him. But it seems they should be more concerned about the outside getting in.

"Apparently," Cypher tells us. "There are also whispers about a jail break, and I do not doubt they'll get it right with the connections they have on the inside. He will never get parole, so it's the only option, and when he gets out, because he will, he'll come after her."

"I don't like it," I tell Cypher.

"Tell me about it," he agrees. "I'll have names and locations in the next hour. I'll send everything over to Falcon." He hangs up before I can ask anything more. But we got all we needed from him for now.

"I want all the details the second it arrives," I tell Falcon.

"Do you think Mahoney is going to get out?" This comes from Hawk, and I can hear the tension in his voice. I don't blame him. The thought of a man who fucked up our lives so badly being free doesn't sit well with me.

"If he is, we'll find him," I promise him. It's a vow. I will make sure the bastard pays, and when he does it will be slow, torturously, and I'll watch with satisfaction when he finally begs for mercy. Because he will.

"I think he'll be the one to find us," Falcon says. "His daughter is in our house, and since he had people tracking her, I have a feeling he's going to pay his little girl a visit the moment he can."

"He won't be able to fly commercial, which means he's going to have private jets carrying him around," I tell Falcon who's already tapping away at his keyboard. With Mahoney's links to the criminal organizations, I don't doubt they'll assist him in crossing borders without being seen.

"The moment any flight lands at any of the air

strips, we'll known about it," Falcon announces, but he doesn't look away from the screen. He could easily sit here all day and not move, whereas I like to be out on the road.

"What was this new job you mentioned?" I ask realizing I didn't hear a word he said about it. I was too focused on Lucille.

"I haven't got all the details yet, but it's an easy one," he says. "Some guy wants the man his wife is cheating with killed." Falcon shrugs. He's right, it's an easy one. "But…" He holds up a finger as he types with one hand, then stops, looks at us, and grins. "The man in question is some famous actor who's doing a tour in the UK for the next three days. We'll have to get to him quickly, and make sure it's public."

"What?" Unease coils in my gut at the request. We don't work in public. We stay in the shadows. "That doesn't sit well with me."

"I know." Falcon nods. "But I have a feeling there may be more to this than meets the eye. I'm going to do a deep dive tonight."

"You mean you're going to sit behind your desk and watch the pretty prisoner in the basement," Hawk retorts as he leans forward, his elbows on his knees. He doesn't say much, but he is perceptive.

"Hey," Falcon starts, "you can't tell me neither of you were going to do the same." I can't deny it, because I was going to watch her for a short time. The cameras in the basement are set up in each corner, giving us a view of the girl. She's going to be intriguing to observe. I know she has a darkness in her, I recognized it the moment she dropped to her knees. When Falcon grabbed her hair, tugging her head back, I saw the desire swimming in the depths of her pretty eyes.

I ignore him as I move out of the office and down the hall. Fighting everything inside me to go down there and make her crawl once more, I ponder what her first task will be. There are so many things I'd love to watch her do while I make her cry, while she bleeds. She'll shed crimson to make up for the past.

As I step into the sanctuary of my bedroom, I can't help smiling.

Nine

LUCILLE

I'M PACING BACK AND FORTH WHEN THE DOOR OPENS. I'VE needed to relieve myself for hours, but no amount of screaming and shouting got me any attention. I know it's a new day since the soft yellow glow of sunshine streaming through the small window in my cell woke me.

When I look up, I find Mr. Silent. I know it's him because of his build, but now he's not wearing the skull faced make up, I can finally see the man underneath. There's a rugged handsomeness to him. His jaw is angular, strong, his eyes are focused as they track me. His lips are full, a deep rose color and his nose is sharp, but there is a slight bump to it which tells me he's been in fights before.

Suddenly, as he takes one step into the room,

I realize I know him. I've seen him before. "You've been following me," I mutter when I realize it's the stranger I bumped into the other night when leaving the pub. "Why?" It's a stupid question. It's obvious why, they wanted to kidnap me.

He doesn't answer me, and I don't expect him to. But he does watch me for a short moment before he turns, leaving the door open. It must be a trick. If I tried to run, he'll catch me and possibly hurt me, or kill me. I don't doubt this man was trained for it.

Tentatively, I take steps toward the threshold, and cautiously walk out into a darkened hallway. He's standing a few feet away, and when he sees I'm following, he turns and walks on further. The deeper into the darkness we go, the more my fight or flight instinct toy with me.

But then he opens another door, and brightness blinds me for a moment. It's a bathroom. Being under the house, which is why I'm guessing it's so dark down here, this is rather clean and sterile looking.

"Freshen up," he grunts, "You have ten minutes." It's all he says before he shuts the door, leaving me in the room which looks like it's been built specifically for clean-up. There aren't any luxuries, only a shower which can fit one person, along with a basin and a small mirror. Everything is white. The wall and floor tiles, and the bright bulb hanging from the ceiling only illuminates this fact even more.

I quickly move to the toilet and relieve my bladder which feels pleasurable, and I can't help but sigh. Once I'm done, I wash my hands and splash my face with warm water. Then I rinse my mouth with the small bottle of mouthwash perched on the edge of the basin.

I don't have a towel to use if I were to shower, so I'll have to forgo the luxury for now. Hopefully they'll allow me to shower later. Looking in the mirror, I can't help but stare at the girl reflecting back at me. I'm not sure how this has happened, but my father has a lot to answer for. He stole so much, and here he is, taking my life without even being in the same fucking country.

Anger surges through me, holding me in its feral grip. I don't want to die, and I don't want to be some sex slave for these assholes, but maybe I can figure out a way to get through to one of them. Maybe the one with the green eyes, Falcon. he seemed less threatening, but even as I think it, I recall his words from last night.

Please, say it again so I can show you what happens to disobedient pets.

An ice-cold shiver trickles down my spine, reminding me I'm not at all safe with him. Perhaps the quiet one will be able to see past the anger and vengeance so clear in their demeanors.

The door opens, startling me and *blue eyes* leans against the frame. Those endless depths seem to bore right through me. "I'm Hawk," he tells me then in a bored tone. "You met Falcon and Crow last night," he continues when I don't respond. "I'm going to take you up to the house now. If you try anything, make no fucking mistake, I'll end you."

My whole body trembles in fear. There is no amusement in his eyes. He isn't lying when he tells me this, and all I can do is swallow. With one rough hand, he grips my arm and drags me down the hall, the opposite way to the bathroom, and I find there's a hidden door which slides open and before us is a set of steps.

Hawk shoves me forward, and I stumble onto the cold concrete. I know what's expected of me, and as tears burn my eyes, I slowly crawl up the steps. He doesn't tell me to stand, he doesn't order me to walk, so I stay kneeling when I reach the main level of the house.

The sunshine is higher now, and it streams through the windows. I look up and find we're in a kitchen. It's a country style, with brass pots and pans hanging from dark metal rods which have been lowered from the high ceiling.

An island made of thick, heavy wood sits below them, and I picture a large work surface waiting for me to start preparing their food. I'm a fucking maid. But I know it's not the only reason I'm here. They want me here for their deviant desires, and those other options leaves unease coiling in my stomach.

"On your feet," Hawk grumbles as he tugs me to stand. "Breakfast." It's the only word he offers before he leaves me in the kitchen. Thankfully it's warmer up here, and I pad over to the radiator which offers me solace for a short moment.

"Nice to have something pretty to look at in the morning," Falcon's voice comes from behind me. I'm startled at the fact he's so good looking. There's a mischievousness to his expression. "We take our coffee black, strong, and we like a big breakfast," he informs me. But I'm still in awe of him. He's inked from under his chin, all the way down to I'm guessing his stomach because the tank top he's wearing hides most of his body.

I was right when I thought of him as leaned, yet strong. His arms are toned, showing off biceps and forearms which make me want to touch them. Shaking my head, I fight back the scoff of stupidity crawling through me. It's ridiculous to think any of them are hot, but I can't deny, if they didn't kidnap me, if I were some random girl, I would definitely be flirting.

"I'm expected to cook?" I throw out, swallowing back the desire burning through my veins. I watch as he moves through the kitchen, where he grabs a large mug from one of the cupboards and fills it with coffee from a pot.

"You're expected to do anything we tell you to, Goldilocks," he responds before sipping the steaming liquid. He doesn't flinch, but I can tell it's hot.

"Can you tell me what my father did to you?" I don't want to know because I've heard the horror stories of the serial killer who would invade homes where there was a babysitter alone with the kids. I was one of those sitters, and it broke me when I realized the monster before me was my own flesh and blood.

Falcon stares at me for a long moment, before he chuckles. "I don't think you're quite ready for that yet, darling," he says. "When you do learn about us, when you come to realize what you're paying for, you'll want to surrender and beg for mercy."

Folding my arms across my chest, I pin my glare on him. "I know he's a monster, I never denied it. I was one of the victims—"

"Don't you dare fucking say another word," the deep, rumble of Crow comes from nowhere, and when he appears in the kitchen like a shadow, my breath catches in my throat. If I thought the other two men were handsome, Crow is a sculpture right out of a gallery. They're all unique in their looks, and

Crow is no different.

His pitch black hair matches his clothes. His tanned, smooth skin looks soft and my fingertips tingle. His lips are full, the top one forming a perfect Cupid's bow, while the lower one, thicker and more prominent makes me want to bite it. His sharp jawbone, along with his perfect nose make up a face that would make the Gods weep. Then there are his eyes—metal, silver, cold.

"You should be making breakfast," he commands in a tone which belies his calm expression. He doesn't fist his hands, he doesn't seem to be angry, but his words are laced with a fury so dangerous, I gulp. He turns to Falcon then. "Meet me in the office." Then he turns and leaves taking all the air from the room.

"Don't upset the main man," Falcon teases with a wink before he disappears after Crow. When I look down, I realize my hands are trembling. I've never come across a man so angry. I can't imagine what my father did to them, but it must have been bad because they've obviously followed me to England. Their American accents are obvious, so I wonder how long they've been planning this.

I turn my attention to the kitchen once more and attempt to focus on cooking them something to eat. My own stomach grumbles in response to the food I find sitting in the fridge. Everything is fresh, the fruit bright and colorful, milk delivered by a milkman, not store bought. Eggs are laid out in a small tray in the door, while there is also a selection of cheeses.

I grab what I need, transferring it to the counter and get to work. I lose myself in the warmth of the stove while I fry up scrambled eggs. It's not great, but I'm not a good cook. Never have been. I survived on ramen and toast for most of the time I'd been here. Thankfully, the pub down the road always did a special dinner treat and I'd end up eating there when I was tired of noodles.

I don't expect to impress them with my skills in the kitchen, but as I start the toast, my mind flicks back to the past, and I recall a moment in time when I didn't know my dad was a monster.

"Please," I beg him. It's going to be my birthday in only two days, and he hasn't told me what he has planned. The man who I look up to, my hero, stands in the living room while my mom sits in her armchair knitting. I always tell her she's too young to knit, she teases me and tells me it keeps her calm.

Our life is perfect. I have a loving family, I have friends and when I turn thirteen, I'm going to start babysitting. But Dad's new job has taken him away so many times in the past few months, I'm scared he's going to miss my special day.

"Don't bother your father," Mom says, but she's grinning from ear to ear.

Dad drops to his knees in front of me. I'll be a teenager, but he still at times talks to me as if I were a child. "I might have to go away for a few days. But listen to me, Cherry Pie," he murmurs, "I'll be back and I'm going to bring you the best present ever."

I don't want to show him how sad it makes me he'll be gone, but I can't hide the expression which must be clear on my face. Dad's smile morphs into guilt, and my chest tightens. I know he has to work to put me through school and pay for our food and such, but I want him here.

I wish he didn't have to leave so much. But Mom said his new boss is strict and doesn't like when things don't go his way. I love my dad, but I think he needs a new boss.

"Okay," I finally mumble, and he pulls me into his arms and holds me tight.

"I love you, Cherry Pie," he whispers in my ear before pressing a kiss to my cheek. "Always."

At the time, he was already a criminal. We learned through the trial how my father started working for the Bratva, then he moved onto the Cartel. All these organizations named are responsible for violence across the world. My father enjoyed what he did.

Sitting in court, I watched him with rapt attention. Satisfaction was painted on his face, as if he knew one day he'd go down, and he wasn't concerned. A shiver traces itself down my spine, as if a finger is slowly trailing me from neck to tailbone.

Guilty. The word rung through the court, and when it was over, when they took him away, he looked right at me. It was as if he was silently telling me he'll come for me.

Deep down, as dangerous as I know my captors are, these three men have nothing on the monster who made me.

Ten
FALCON

Since the email came through from Dante, I'm wondering how to make this shit go away. I read through the details this morning, I know I have to tell Crow, but as he watches me from his desk, I'm concerned.

He's on edge. It's because of her. Having her so close, in our home, it's taking a toll on him. It's been eight hours, more or less, and yet I've seen the tension in his shoulders tighten with every passing moment.

But fuck me, she's beautiful. I can't stop thinking about her either. Last night, I watched her from my computer, knowing soon enough, I'll have her naked, taking my dick.

"What's going on with the intel from Savage?"

Crow questions, his gaze zeroed in on mine.

Leaning back in the chair, I kick my feet out and say, "We've found the links, like he said on the call. But what he did find is Mahoney made a call to the Bratva; he wants them to get him out."

"Without the prospect of parole, there is only one way of him getting out," Crow says, and I nod. The fucker is going to break out. "If he steps foot outside those walls, he's fair game. The girl will die before him though," he tells me.

"Does she though?" We planned our revenge for years, but right now, I don't know if I want to kill her. Hurt her yes, make her cry and scream, most definitely. But to slice such a pretty throat has me second guessing myself.

"Yes," Crow grunts. "There's no other way. That filthy blood ends with her. She will not give birth to another monster."

"But if we get him, then I don't see—"

"Are you wanting out on this plan?" Crow's angry, silver glare pins me to the chair. I open my mouth, then shut it. I want to say yes, but I can't let my brothers down.

"No," I finally answer him. "I think if we can get her father in the chamber and make him pay, what's the use in hurting her?"

"He can watch as she is tainted by three men." The corner of Crow's mouth tilts upward. The idea of sharing the beauty with my brothers makes my dick jolt against my jeans. "He can witness her violation, as she begs for mercy from the pain we'll cause her, and when we're done, he'll be the one begging us to stop."

I've always known Crow was fucked, I don't blame him, I am too, but his words instill unease in my gut. "What if she's innocent?"

"She's his daughter." I can tell I'm not going to get through to Crow, not now. Perhaps he's right. I may be letting my dick think for me. When my best friend glares at me, I want to take back my words.

"There are many innocent people who died; children were killed," Crow insists, and I can't fight him on this because. "Don't you remember what he did to your family?" His question slowly sinks into my mind. I don't have to nod because he settles back as he takes in the expression on my face. There is no denying it, my anger is still present.

"If this bastard gets out, he will come for her," I tell Crow, not bothering to respond to his query. "We can track him down easily, and the moment he steps foot on a plane, we'll know."

He nods. "Another thing," Crow says, before he pushes to his feet. "I don't want her sleeping up here yet."

"Why?"

"I don't trust her." I understand his concern.

She'll end up trying to escape, and I have no doubt Crow will end her before she even makes it to the property line. We have a large expanse of a garden, but there's nothing around us for miles. The closest neighbor is fifty miles away, which means our little captive won't make it very far.

"I don't either."

"But you were ready to save her a minute ago. Or were you thinking with your dick?" His challenge makes me laugh out loud. *Bastard.*

"Maybe. Why? Jealous?"

Crow rounds the desk and stalks toward me. His eyes blaze with intent when he reaches me and stops inches from where I'm standing. He leans in, brushing his lips against mine. The heat of him scorches me, sending desire shooting through every nerve ending in my body.

"Do I have to be?" His whisper feathers over my mouth, and when he reaches around to tangle his fingers in my growing hair, he fists the short strands and tugs my head back. The wet warmth of his tongue laps along the column of my neck, over my Adam's apple, right up to my chin.

"Never," I finally respond, before his lips capture mine. My cock throbs when his tongue duels mine. The kiss is rough and urgent, dripping with unconstrained need. It's been a while since we played, and I think having *her* here has made us all ravenous.

I grip his hips in a vise-like hold and tug him against me. His hardness against mine. The clothing covering our flesh causing blissful friction. The office door creaks open, but Crow doesn't pull away until a soft feminine gasp echoes through the air.

When we break our kiss, I turn to find Lucille on the threshold, her eyes wide as saucers, and her mouth popped open into an O. Surprise paints her features, and I can't deny, she is a pretty girl.

"I-I-I'm—"

"You're enjoying the show?" I taunt, causing a soft red to color her cheeks. Her flesh is smooth, blemish free, and I wonder how easy it would be to mark her up. "Come here."

She hesitates for a moment but thinks twice when her gaze lands on Crow who hasn't moved. He's still inches from me. His cock presses against my ass, and I'm tempted to grind back against him. But my focus is on the girl.

The moment she steps up to me, I reach out for her, causing her to wince. But I don't slap her, not yet. The thought makes me smile, and I can read the wariness on Lucille's face. With one swift movement, I tip her head to the side, before running my thumb over the pulse point which is currently thrumming as she regards me.

"You're nervous."

"I've been kidnapped, held in a basement, and been told I need to obey," she whispers as I tease her silky smooth flesh. The more I touch her, the faster Crow's breath gets behind me. Then, without warning, I grip her neck, the delicate column small in my large hand.

I don't choke her yet, but I don't miss how her pupils dilate. She enjoys rough; she loves the feeling of being taken. I bet if I were to force her to her knees and shoved my cock down her throat it would make her little cunt wet.

"Open your mouth," Crow commands in a tone of pure anger, which belies the thickness of his erection which is still prominent against me. I smile when Lucille obeys him. Tears form in her eyes when he steps around me and inches toward her. She's more afraid of him than of me, I can't have that.

My fingers dig into the sides of her esophagus, and I squeeze. Crow knows what I'm doing, and he wastes no time in sliding two fingers into her mouth, along her tongue. He pushes all the way to the back until our pretty Goldilocks gags. Her throat works to swallow him, while I squeeze the breath from her lungs. Fuck, the thought of having my cock in there while she's struggling to breath makes me throb.

Crow doesn't relent. He continues his ministrations while his head is tipped to the side in fascination. He's enjoying himself. There's a hint of a smile on his lips. He reaches up with his free hand and pinches her pretty pixie nose closed. Those beautiful eyes widen in shock, realization hitting her, and she starts to struggle.

But as Hawk enters the room, I know he'll join in our little game. His hands wrap around her wrists, and he holds them behind her back. Lucille becomes nothing more than a gurgling mess. Spit drips from her plump lips, down her chin. It wets her top, and I wish she was naked before us.

It's been a while since I was this turned on. After my kiss with Crow, and now this, I'm close to coming in my fucking jeans. He pulls his fingers from her mouth, wet with saliva before he slowly leans in. He makes sure she watches as he places both digits in his mouth and licks them clean.

"You're nothing more than a filthy toy," he whispers with venom in his tone. His hatred runs deep, more so than I thought. "I'm going to make every day you spend in our home a nightmare. You'll beg me for mercy, you'll fucking break under me," he warns her while we hold her steady.

Then, he shoves his fingers down her throat once more, and I feel her neck work furiously, it doesn't take much for me to figure out what he wants from her. I release her neck and step back. Not a moment too soon and Lucille drops to her knees and heaves.

All I can do is thank God Crow didn't have

carpet in his office. The cool wooden floor beneath our prisoner must be harsh on her knees. But if I had to be honest, seeing her there, only makes my cock harder than ever.

"Clean it up," Crow orders as he leaves her on the floor and gets back to his work.

I glance up to look at Hawk. I can't tell what he's thinking, usually I can, but right now, his face is devoid of all emotion. I'm not sure what's going on, but he turns and leaves.

"I'm going to check on him," I tell Crow. I shouldn't leave Lucille alone in here with him, but I'm worried about Hawk. We're close, all three of us, and when one is struggling, we all band together.

When I reach him, he's in the living room, leaning on the patio doors which slide open and offer a pathway to the enormous garden. His hands on the glass, as he looks out toward the back of the property.

"What's going on?"

"I can't be here, with her so close," he mumbles after a long, silent moment. "Touching her makes me livid. I can't stop picturing the moment everything went down. She was there."

"There?" I'm so confused. Hawk has been the only one of us who never admitted what he saw the night Lucille's father broke into their home. Crow and I both know what the news channels reported, and I've never hacked into the records to read up on them myself. Even if I did, it wouldn't give me what I want—the story through Hawk's eyes.

He drops his head and his shoulders bunch up with the tension clearly twisting him up inside. I want to go to him, but I know if I do, I'm only going to end up with a bloody nose. When he's in this kind of mindset, it's best to have him come to me.

As minutes pass, and the silence gets thicker, I'm almost certain he's not going to speak, but then, a murmur comes from him. "Most of the night is still a blur of sirens and flashing lights." His voice is distant, as if he's back there, witnessing whatever horror he saw. "But before, when it was dark and quiet, I saw an angel."

Now I'm convinced the guy has lost his mind. "What? Were you drinking?" Even my usual taunts don't lighten the heavy mood which has taken over the room.

"An angel with golden hair and flawless skin," he whispers. Then, without warning, he spins around to pin me with a pained glare. "Lucille was in my house the night of the murder, or kidnapping." My stomach drops to the ground. My lungs give out, breath knocked from them completely. I open my mouth to respond, to ask questions, but none come out.

I can tell he's waiting for me to say something.

Hawk is a man of not many words, and even now, when he drops this bombshell, he's quietly going through whatever the fuck he's going through. "She was the babysitter?" I know she was sitting for Crow's folks when her father struck, but I didn't realize she worked for Hawk's parents too.

"No." The word is a resounding omen which has every hair on the back of my neck standing to attention. This makes no sense, if she didn't work for them, what was she doing there. "I need to think," Hawk announces quickly before rushing from the living room. I watch him go, still trying to process.

I need to find out more.

I'm going to have to break our code and look into Hawk's case. I don't want to, but if Crow finds out, he'll kill her without trying to find out the truth.

Something tells me our little Goldilocks must be guilty too.

Eleven
CROW

Hate fuels me daily. She's going to pay for everything she's done—including making me want to taste her smooth, silky flesh. Watching her clean my floor hasn't stopped my hard on from throbbing. I'm behind my desk, attempting to focus on work, but I can't stop my gaze from straying toward her.

When she finally rises to her feet, I stop what I'm doing and lean back in my chair. She's filled with rage. I like it on her, it makes her more beautiful. Something about a woman who is willing to fight back makes my dick hard.

"I'm done," she announces before picking up the bucket of water she used to clean up the mess she made. The image of her taking my fingers is still fresh in my mind, and looking at her lips now, I want so much to see my cock sliding between them. "Anything else?"

Her question has my gaze lifting to her eyes. "Your clothes are a mess," I inform her. "Take them off." I've always enjoyed control; I've honed the skill and I consider myself an expert.

Her mouth pops open. "What?"

"You heard me," I say before waving my hand toward her. "Take them off." It's a simple order, one she can't refuse. Well, she can, but then she'll learn the consequences. I don't like repeating myself, but more so, I don't like having to wait. When I ask for something, I expect it done and without question.

"I can't just—"

"I've seen naked women before, little mouse," I tell her with a smirk. "I doubt you have anything special I want to see." I push to my feet, and I'm so tempted to slice the damn material from her body. Or rip it with my bare fucking hands. And I will. I want her to gasp, to fear me. I want her to feel exactly what I did when she let her monster of a father take my brothers.

"Why are you doing this?"

"I told you why." I keep my voice controlled, steeled with anger. It's the only way to get through life. No other emotion exists. Because the moment you allow feelings like love and affection in, or even empathy, you get hurt. So, instead of going through any heartbreak again, I have focused solely on the anger, the rage; it warms my blood and keeps me alive.

The *thing* in my chest pumping oxygen to my body, the cold, unused organ comes alive.

Lucille looks up at me as I near her. She's a tiny thing, her head reaching my chest. When I stop inches from her, I don't miss the wince creasing her face or the flash of fear which dances in her eyes. Beautiful golden orbs filled with anxious flames.

"I don't… I think—"

"You're not here to think," I say before I grip the front of her sleep shirt and tug, causing her to stumble toward me. Her body flush with mine, shakes like a leaf. A soft gasp tumbles from her pink lips, and my cock jolts against my zipper. "You feel that?"

I roll my hips, grinding my dick right up against her soft belly. Need races through my veins as her warmth wafts over me. I wonder briefly if she's wet, if her cunt is smooth, or trimmed. I want to find out.

"That's because I can't stop thinking about making you cry. I can't get the image of you choking on my fingers out of my mind, and each time I see it in my mind's eye, my cock weeps for more."

"You're sick," she bites out, finding her fire, and I have to admit, even to myself, it's an aphrodisiac. I want more. I want her to burn me right down to the bone. I want to do the same to her, I want to shatter every inch of her.

"I know," I acquiesce with a smile. "But you know all about sick men. Don't you, little mouse?" Guilt flashes in her eyes. She knows I'm talking about her father. But she doesn't know I've seen her little online chat room. I know all about her dirty needs. I want to appease them. I want to dance with her demons.

"Let me go," Lucy pleads with me. I want her begging, but not to be released.

Ignoring her, I grip the top she's wearing and tug with both hands, the material making a satisfying rip right down the middle. Her tits fall out to my gaze. The mounds a handful with dark nipples that look like they're in need of attention. Peaks of flesh have my mouth watering.

Without saying a word, she shoves her pajama pants down her thighs, and soon, she's before me in nothing more than a pair of panties. The black cotton not what I was expecting, and I smile.

"See," I say. "Was that so difficult?"

She's uncomfortable. Her body trembles as she stands before me. Every inch of her is smooth, soft, and I can only imagine how she tastes.

"Is this what you like?" Lucy whispers gently. The pain in her tone gives me pause, but it only lasts a short moment before I offer her a smirk. "Do you like women being scared of you? Looking at you as if you were a monster?" Her snide remarks only seem to make me want to listen to her some more.

"I thought you liked monsters," I throw back, arching a brow as I regard her with curious desire. I can't fight this need I have to fuck her, but I also hate her and the blood she comes from.

"Don't ever think you know anything about me because I can tell you right now, you don't. You're a little boy wanting to play games," Lucile spits as anger drenches her words and I can't stop my hand from moving. The slap causes my palm to sting, and a gasp of shock echoes around me. Her eyes glisten with tears and her delicate fingers reach for the dark pink handprint on her cheek.

"If you ever talk to me like that again—"

"What? You'll punch me? Hit me again?" She spins on her heel and makes her way for the door, but I don't go after her. Instead, I stare at the empty doorway for far too fucking long.

I've always been too proud to apologize; the word *sorry* isn't in my vocabulary, but as she disappears from my office, I mumble, "Sorry."

I'm still standing on the same spot when Hawk walks into the office. His gaze tracks me, then lowers to the material on the floor. When those blue eyes snap back to mine, questions dance in them.

"Take her back to the basement," I say, before turning to my desk.

He ignores me, and asks, "What did you do?"

I don't know what I fucking did. When I'm near her, all I want is to see her cry. I want to hurt her. It's the only thing keeping me sane. I've held onto my pain for so long, I don't know how else to survive. She can't change it or I will lose my mind.

"Crow?" Hawk's voice breaks through the cloud hanging over me, and I finally shake my head. "What happened?"

"I slapped her," I admit, "I liked it. I wanted to make her cry and she did. Her eyes shone with tears, pain, grief. All the things we've felt for so long."

He doesn't care. I know he doesn't. Something Hawk hasn't allowed himself to do for a long time is to allow empathy into his mind. I don't blame him. I've shut off my emotions as well. But the fighter in him usually takes over when we're on a job. This is one of our most important jobs yet. "And?"

"And I want to do it again," I confess, but my voice is free of any guilt. I thought it would be easier than this, but looking at Lucille, there's a light inside her, one which seems to outshine everything I thought I wanted.

Hawk shrugs as he looks at me and asks, "Are you sure you want to go through with this?" There's no doubt I do. But he's checking up on me. It's part of our promise, we always told each other we would do check-ups when we thought it was needed. What we each experienced in our own way has changed us. When we lose ourselves in those memories, it can take a toll, more than normal.

I look up at him and smile. "Of course," I finally say. My head is clear once more. Whatever shit she pulled on me, it's gone. I can see again. "She will die, no matter what."

Hawk looks at me skeptically, and I know he's trying to figure out what happened. I can't explain it. I've never once said the word and yet, she dragged it out of me.

"I want her in the basement. Feed her, give her water, or juice, whatever, but I don't want her in our space. She's not ready," I inform him. "Keep her down there for a few days as we needle our way into her mind. I wanted to do this faster, but we need to take our time with her."

"What about Falcon?"

"I don't give a shit what Falcon wants," I bite out, frustration taking a hold of me. I fist my hands and release them to calm the tension coursing through me. She's only been here for one fucking day and already I'm losing my shit.

"Okay." Hawk's sigh is loud and fucking clear. I'm not changing my mind. The plan was to bring her here, to show her what a monster her father is, and then, to lure him right into our trap.

One thing didn't make sense when the cases were being investigated, and it had to do with Lucille. I'm not sure what they were hiding, but the cops seemed to have had more intel than they were giving us. When I asked Falcon to look into it, he couldn't find anything. It's been buried, and it's been buried fucking deep.

Sitting back, I listen to the sounds of the house, my focus is shot to hell now. Hawk's deep rumble travels down the hall to my office followed by the biting tone of our prisoner. She's a handful in more ways than one. I don't see them pass by which means he's taken her down to the basement. We'll have to keep her down there for a while. She's too fucking fired up to be up here. I don't need her breaking our shit.

I have a feeling she will throw a tantrum if left to her own devices. I shut my eyes and lean my head against the soft leather of my chair. A picture of her fills my mind, and those slight curves of smooth flesh make me groan. I want to run my fingertips over her skin before I slide my blade over the same trail.

The only part of her I haven't seen is her pretty cunt. I don't doubt it's beautiful, like the fucking rest of her. God how I want to see her bleed. To watch crimson rivulets dot every inch of her would be nothing short of euphoric.

Not only because I love playing with blood, tasting it, feeling it against me when I'm fucking a woman. But also because it will ensure she suffers pain while I bestow pleasure on her.

By the time we're done with her, she'll crave us. She'll beg us not to end her life. But the road to that day will be an uphill battle.

"Crow," Falcon's voice drags me from my thoughts, and I open my eyes to find him at my door. "We have something." He enters, holding a printout which he sets in front of me the moment he gets to my desk.

I scan the document he's set in front of me and every drop of blood currently racing through my veins turns to ice. My fist crunches the page as I glance up to find Falcon looking at me as if he's going to have to fight me on this. Confidence sparks in his eyes.

"She's going to die," I tell him without flinching. Earlier, I had my doubts. I thought perhaps I was wrong, it only lasted for a second or two, but it happened. When I said sorry to her. But after this, there is no more apologies. "The plan is on, and I don't give a shit what anyone says."

"I'm with you," he tells me. I've seen Falcon angry; I've seen him hurt, but I've never seen him like this before. I'm usually the one to fly off the handle, but this time, I have a feeling Falcon is going to be the one to start our plan. He's going to set it in motion, and he's going to enjoy every fucking moment. "Do we tell Hawk?"

"Tell me what?"

We both snap our gazes to our brother, and I realize we need to tell him the truth of what we have found. There is no more running away. I wish we didn't have to do this. It's going to break him. But he needs to know.

"Falcon found something." My voice is low, controlled, as I slide the crumpled page over my desktop. I let the cards fall where they may.

Twelve
HAWK

I DIDN'T THINK ANGER COULD TAKE A HOLD OF ME LIKE this, but it has, and I'm lost to it. Falcon and Crow watch me. They know this is a game changer. I'm silent for too long, but I can't find the words. I've struggled since *that* night.

"I'm going out," I announce. They know where I'm going, there is no need to ask questions, and there is certainly no need to follow, but Falcon does. Crow has always been more understanding of my needs because he has his own. Falcon takes a calmer approach to situations which hurt him, anger him, I've never been able to do it. "I don't need a babysitter," I grit through clenched teeth.

He's trying to help when his hand lands on my shoulder, stopping me. I spin on my heel, ready to take him down when Falcon grabs my face in his hands and pulls me toward him. His lips find mine, and we kiss. Teeth gnashing at plump lips. The need to devour is strong, it takes a hold of me and doesn't let go.

When Falcon finally breaks the kiss, his gaze locks on mine. "Don't do stupid shit," he tells me. "Let's go down there and question the girl."

"If I go near her right now, I'll hurt her," I admit. I've never hit a woman, never touched one in anger, but with her, knowing what I do now, I can't deny I'm tempted to make her cry.

"I'll be with you," Falcon assures me, his hands still holding me steady. I wonder if I should. I know running away from problems is not the way to solve them. We need her to know what we've been through. I have to tell her my story at some point, but right now, all I can see is the deception in those angelic features. There's a light in her and I'm dying to snuff it out. I want her to be in pain.

"And what if you can't stop me?" I ask him earnestly. There have been times in the ring where I was convinced I could kill again. Not as a job, but for fun. In the past, it was required of me, but then I got lost to it. The sense of satisfaction I found when I watched the light die in someone's eyes, it was euphoric.

"You know I'll kick your ass," Falcon tells me,

but there's a guarded fear in his eyes. He doesn't want to believe I'll hurt her, but the fact he's not one hundred percent sure shows on his face.

"Falc," I whisper. "I want to, I really do."

"Then stop fighting me, trust me to be there for you," he pleads, it's affectionate, more so than I deserve. But I nod anyway. He smiles then, it's bright on his face. He's the joker of the three of us.

"Are you two done cuddling now?" Crow questions as he pushes off the wall he'd been leaning on.

"Fuck you," both Falcon and I bite out, but there's a lightheartedness to the room. The tension has lifted, even if momentarily. But I ask, "Are we all going down there?"

"Yes," Crow affirms with a nod. "We're in this together. I'm not letting you go down there alone." He may be the colder one of the three of us, but there's still love in his heart. It only comes in the form of firm words and a swift nod, but it's there.

We move silently through the house until we reach the steps taking us down to the basement. The echoes of our footsteps will alert her of her impending doom, but she doesn't know how much I want to see her bleed right now.

The documentation confirms what I always thought. At first, I figured I was going crazy. It wasn't possible, but it most definitely is. There is no other explanation for it, Lucille was with her father that night.

She wasn't only a victim, but she stood beside him when he tortured the one person I loved more than anyone else. Even my folks would joke around about me caring more about my sister than them, because it was true. I took being an elder brother seriously. There was only a year between us, she was mine to look after.

By the time we reach the basement, every inch of my body is thrumming, as if an electric current is running right though me. The door creaks open, and on the bed, is the angelic blonde.

"On your feet," Crow demands, his tone rigid.

She doesn't ignore him this time. I'm certain it has something to do with the fact he slapped her. Fear can make people submit so easily. It's beautiful to watch. He drags the chair over the concrete floor, making sure to have the sound bounce off the walls. Lucille's wince is clear as he sets it in the center of the room.

"Sit."

Once more, she obeys without argument. I watch in awe as he binds her ankles to either side of the chair, her legs spread. She's dressed in a T-shirt I gave her since Crow discarded her pajamas. Her body may be covered, but I can't stop my mind from recalling the smooth flesh of her luscious tits. How her nipples peaked.

"What are you going to do to me?" Her voice is a broken whisper of worry. Those beautiful eyes shimmer as she looks up at him. Once her hands are bound behind her back, Crow stops before her, crouching down until they're eye to eye.

"I'm going to ask you a series of questions," he informs her. "Hawk here will administer any punishment he deems fitting."

"Punishment? For what?" The surprise on her face is clear.

"Tell us something, Lucille," Crow starts, as I move in behind him. I want to see the look on her face as he asks the questions. "When did you learn your father was a monster?"

"What?"

"When?"

The tears shimmering in her eyes, hanging onto her lashes, fall when she blinks. The wet trail trickling down her cheeks makes me want to see more of the same. I want her salty emotion to soak her smooth skin until she's nothing more than a blubbering mess.

"I-I was working as a sitter," she whispers, and we watch as her lashes flutter, but Crow won't stand for her looking away. I'm right in my thoughts when his hands snatches her chin, forcing her to open her eyes and look at him.

"You face us as you speak," he grits, his thumb and forefinger squeezing the flesh in his grip. He doesn't allow guilt to rule his actions, he doesn't allow affection to take a hold and stop him from doing what he needs to.

"I was working as a sitter, for a few families in the city," Lucille speaks now, her watchful gaze flicking between us. "I was fifteen when I started, I grew to love the families I worked for."

"And what was your father doing at the time?" We're finally going to get the answers we have searched for since we were barely eighteen. It's been too long. We'd all left home to study abroad. When Falcon's mom called to tell us about the horrors our families had gone through, we went home. We raced home.

I need answers about what occurred the moment I walked into my house and

saw her standing beside her father as he took what wasn't his to take.

"H-He worked away from home most months," Lucille admits. "We hardly saw him most times, and when we did, he was distant." Her gaze lands on mine, and for a moment, I want to believe her. I want her to be innocent in all this, but she's not.

The police report confirms she was present, she never worked for my family, but she was in my home. The link though doesn't make sense.

Granted, we lived on the same street, but my folks never wanted a babysitter.

Why would she have been there if not to help him?

"Why were you at my house that night?" I ask, my voice rough with pain as I recall the moment she turned her head and looked right at me. I was mostly in the shadows, but she would have seen me standing there.

"I-I…" Lucille shakes her head for a moment. "I don't remember," she tells me, her eyes holding mine. Every nerve in my body wants to attack. "I don't ever remember being there," she says and I lose all control and lunge at her.

My hand fits around her throat easily. The delicate column fragile against my touch, and her pulse riots as I squeeze the air from her lungs.

I lean forward, my nose almost touches hers. The warmth of her worried breaths making my body ache for more. To do more. "Do not lie to me," I hiss in her face. "I saw you that night, standing beside him and you looked right at me."

I don't give her time to speak. My head is spinning with the scent of her. She may not have showered in two days, there's still a sweetness wafting from her and it makes my cock hard, and my brain consider all the things I could do to her.

"I-I…" she croaks once more, and I let up my hold on her neck. "You don't remember everything," she tells me as the tears continue to fall. Her words though, they give me a pause.

"What do you mean?"

My brothers are behind me, listening to every word. They all need to know what the fuck is going on. I want the truth and I want it now, or I will start hurting her, and she won't like it. I'll make sure every inch of her smooth, pale flesh is tainted with me.

"H-h-he had bound my hands in front of my body," Lucy whispers, the words pained with the memory of her monster. She shakes her head slowly before looking me in the eye, "He had a knife to my throat."

"You're lying." My mouth goes dry as I try to recall the night with more clarity. I believed I knew what happened that night, what I saw. *But is it possible I've been hiding certain aspects of the memories? Have I buried it so deep nothing makes sense anymore?*

"I'm not," she tells me confidently. Her eyes shine and the wetness o her cheeks make her look ethereal. Confusion twists in my gut. "He came home angry that night," she continues when I don't answer. My hand slowly falls away as I try to figure out what the fuck is going on in my head. "He was drunk, and dragged me from the house with my mother screaming at him to leave me alone. By then, she knew about the Bratva," Lucille admits. "I still didn't understand it."

Shock must be painted on my face because the pain in her eyes dances like flames in the darkness. "Your mother knew?"

Lucille nods slowly. "She found some papers in his office, and when she questioned him, he took me. He told her I would see what I have to look forward to in a few years."

"What did he mean?" I ask, my shoulders tense, my gut coiling like a serpent, readying its attack. "Did he tell you what the fuck he was doing this shit for?"

"Hawk—"

"No," I spit as I regard Crow from over my shoulder. "She needs to fucking tell us the truth right now. I'm done waiting." I've completely lost all control, and it's all because of her. She shouldn't be here because I can't trust myself around her. She's dangerous not only to me, but to my brothers as well. I won't let her blood taint us any longer. I reach for the rope holding her arms behind her back and I tug it free before I step behind the chair and slide it around her neck.

"What—"

I cut her words off as I lift her from the chair with the noose and lean in until my lips feather along her earlobe. "Tell me everything, and if you leave anything out, I will know. And you know what happens then?" I don't wait for her to choke out her response, I tighten the rope until she coughs and convulses against me which only seems to make my jeans tighten at the crotch.

My brothers don't stop me. They know I'm not thinking straight, and if they come near me right now, I will kill her. And I won't think twice about doing it.

When I finally release her, Lucille slumps into the chair and sputters while drawing in much needed breaths. I'm in front of her in an instant, and I watch her rub those slender fingers along the column of her neck which is now turning a deep shade of red.

"Now," I say, "Let's start from the beginning."

Thirteen
LUCILLE

I SHOULD BE ANGRY. BUT I'M NOT. THESE MEN HAVE BEEN tortured by my father, and now I'm here because they need to know why I went with him to his last job before he got caught. It was my fault my dad is behind bars. If I didn't fight him at the car, the cops would never have caught up with us.

Taking a deep breath, I look at each man and start my story. "When I was fifteen, I started babysitting. My father wasn't happy about it, but my mother said I should learn to earn my own money. Responsibility. He never agreed with her because he believed I would be married off to the highest bidder."

"By then he was already knee-deep in business with the Bratva. Although, we had no idea. It was only when he used to do long trips, return, and there was something darker about him. It's strange how he changed before my very eyes."

"What do you mean?" Falcon says, the other two men are silent, anger emanating from them as they glare at me. I don't blame them for thinking I was in on it. But they need to understand what went wrong. But before I can even get to my explanation, I need to tell them how I got there.

"He would talk about blood, death, weapons," I tell them. "He didn't seem to be fazed by the violence." It confused me how my father who used to be a calm, affectionate man had changed.

"He liked it," Hawk murmurs and I nod. "Because of his work with the Bratva. But why would he target families you were working for?"

"Easy access," I tell them. "I honestly don't know. I thought perhaps he was trying to get me into trouble when he came to the first house without telling me. But he didn't do it again, and I figured perhaps he forgot I wasn't supposed to allow anyone in the houses when I was sitting for them."

"He was scoping the houses out," Crow says suddenly which surprises me. He's been quiet for a while, and his deep baritone belies the beautiful exterior. His face is shadowed, his black hair falling across his forehead which makes him seem younger than I guess he is.

"Yes." My answer is a whisper of pain and guilt. "He knew how to get in, he knew where the alarms were. Each home I thought was safe, wasn't. The men he worked for, they had connections," I tell them. I recall times when I thought my father was asking about my job because he cared. On my sixteenth birthday, it was the night I witnessed the monster.

"Tell me something," Crow requests, his eyes locked on mine. The silver making every hair on the back of my neck stand on end. There is something so dangerous about him. Not only for my body, but my heart. But when I look at Falcon, I notice it too. Hawk is harder to read, he's more subdued, but each one of them have me wanting to cradle them. I want to hold them and tell them I'm sorry. "The night... The night my brothers—"

I can't stop the tears from falling once more. I was there trying to hold onto the two boys, but I couldn't. My father stabbed me in the back, literally. The wound still clearly visible on my flesh, a silver streak of me fighting back.

"I tried so hard to hold them," I mumble as the tears fall. "He stabbed me." I've never told anyone this before. My mother knew because she was at the hospital with me, but the family didn't know because I left the house, called the police and was taken away before they returned.

"What?" Crow looks down at me. He saw me naked, and he didn't notice it. I stood before him, but he didn't know I was hiding something. "Where?"

I struggle to stand and pull off the T-shirt I'm wearing. "Along my spine," I explain as they all three move swiftly. The silence is heavy with emotion. I didn't think either of these men would ever *feel* anything, but this isn't something they were expecting.

There are times I look in the mirror and wish I was someone else. I pray at night I wake up without a reminder of my reality, but it's always there. I can never escape who I am. I'm the monster's daughter.

Fingertips trace the scar, and I can't help but shiver at the touch. It's gentle, calm. When Hawk rounds me and stops inches from my front, he suddenly grasps my face and pulls me into him. His lips find mine, and he bites my lips, both top and bottom until I'm whimpering in pained need.

Someone is on my left, another on my right, but I can't see because my focus is on the man in front of me. His body is hard, warm, and his tongue invades me like I'm pretty sure his cock would—painfully domineering.

I open for him though because I crave it. When Hawk finally breaks away from me, his gaze is scorching as he regards me. "I want more. I want to know what you were doing in my house that night.

How he brought you there."

I nod, but he holds my head steady.

"We all need to know what happened."

"I know," I tell him. "I can't claim to be a victim like all of you, and your families, but I never once stood by what he did." I need them to believe me because I need to escape them. The thought comes unbidden to me, and I realize in all the time I've been sitting here, the last thing on my mind was getting free.

"You'll stay in here until we're ready for you," Crow announces before he practically drags Hawk from the room. Falcon follows, but before he closes the door to my prison, he winks at me and shuts me inside.

It's only when I'm alone, do I realize I'm no longer bound to the chair. I know no amount of screaming will make them return and let me go. I tried crying out, and shouting for help, but being down here muffles any sounds. So I sit back and allow my tears to fall.

Of all the things my father did to me, this is by far the worst. He didn't touch me, but it's still his doing.

There were many nights I cried myself to sleep. I didn't tell them the shocker. I doubt they would care. All they need is to know why my father did what he did. I understand the need for answers. I can no longer blame them. I never thought I would be able to agree with what they're doing, what they've done, but I do.

I settle back and think about all the times I wondered why I had to be his daughter. Most girls have good dads. They have parents who love and nurture them, not turn them into broken toys to be used and abused at their will.

My father did a lot of things to me, things I don't even want to consider. I wanted to escape, but couldn't, and now I'm a captive once more. The tears fall freely now. They fall in rivulets down my cheeks, the pain of my past taking a hold.

In the cold, I shiver, and I wish they'd given me a warmer top to wear. The one Hawk gave me earlier is thin, and doesn't offer heat. I cry myself to sleep because it's the only way I can find rest. Nothing else will ever bring me calm.

When I wake, I'm lying on the cold hard bed. My body aches in places I didn't think it could ache in. There are no sounds, which means I'm still alone in the dank shit hole they put me in. I turn over and open my eyes, and I find the basement room filled with unnatural light.

"Fuck," I grit as the glare burns my retinas. I

push to sit and take in the room. A groan rumbles in my chest when I stand. A ring light which looks like those influencers use to film videos shines down on me, and a speaker echoes to life in the concrete room.

"She's awake," Falcon's voice tinkles from the corners of my hell.

I glance up, causing my head to spin. Confusion clouds my thoughts, and once again, it's as if I've lost a few days to my life. "How…? What day is it?"

"You've been asleep for about…" he hangs the words in the air, and I wait until he chuckles and tells me, "forty-eight hours."

"Two days?"

"Well," Falcon taunts. "You had some help. We needed you calm for the next step in our plan." There is a nonchalance to him which makes me angry. I told them about my pain, about what I dealt with and they're still treating me like a monster.

"What is going on?"

"I've been told to watch you while those fuckers go and finish a job," he tells me, the satisfaction in his tone makes me want to punch him in the face. He knows he's in control and he's enjoying it far too much.

"I need the restroom," I tell him, hoping he'll show me some mercy.

A chuckle echoes in the room. "Good," he says.

"Then I get to see the princess take a piss."

"You're vile," I bite out as anger takes over the emotions which had thwarted my perception of them the night of my admissions. "I told you what you wanted to know, and now you're treating me as if I were a prisoner."

"You are a prisoner, Goldilocks," Falcon says as he laughs out loud. A buzzing comes from somewhere beside my bed. "I left you a little gift. Feel free to send me nude selfies when I'm not here."

I realize there's a cell phone at my feet, and I pick it up, praying I'll be able to call the police, but the moment I swipe to unlock it, I realize it's locked to all outgoing calls.

"Oh, and don't even bother trying," Falcon informs me. "I've made sure you're only able to contact one of the three of us." Of course he did. When I was upstairs, I got a glimpse into their lives. Falcon is the computer genius, while Crow is the leader. Even though it's not his title officially, he has a commanding presence which holds everyone in the room hostage.

Hawk is the silent killer. I was convinced I was dead when he wrapped his fingers around my neck. The squeeze of them still a phantom tingle on my neck. His fingers long gone, but the memory of them clear as fucking day.

I doubt I'll get out of this house alive. There is

clearly a plan they've concocted to make me pay for my father's sins. I realized the other night, there is no amount of begging to free me from this prison.

"A pretty, yet sad girl," Falcon remarks, dragging me from my thoughts. "How I wish she was naked right now." His laugh vibrates through the speaker, through me. Nothing will bring me greater pleasure than to watch him squirm.

I have never wanted to cause someone pain as much as I do him. It doesn't matter how good looking the bastard is, he's still a fucking asshole. A hot one, but an asshole. Suddenly, the speaker stops and the silence in the room is deafening. The phone in my hand vibrates, and I find a photo from Falcon showing me a thumbs up. I'm not sure if they have cameras in here, but I flash him a middle finger. I have no doubt in my mind he can see me.

The men have no morals. I can't expect them to have any sympathy for me. It doesn't matter that I'm female, I'm still the villain in their story. Or rather my dad is. Which makes me a villain in their books.

It's interesting how life works. You can either be the hero or the villain in someone's story, depending on how and by who the story is being told.

Fourteen
CROW

Each time I've wanted to go down there, I haven't. Falcon set up the cameras, the speakers, and yet, I've yet to venture away from my computer. Work is my focus. But she's in my peripheral. I want answers, but I also don't want them. What she told us the other night was enough to anger me even more. Perhaps she's ready to come upstairs, to listen to our stories.

I wanted her dead, but after what she told us, I'm more intrigued by the girl. It's why I've kept my distance. My plan has gone to shit because I never expected to *want* to know more about her. She was a means to an end. But it seems this pretty girl has needled her way into my mind.

Pushing away from my desk, I make my way

down the hall. Falcon is in his office, the door closed, while Hawk is out. He's been running solo for the past few days. He hasn't ventured down to see her again, and I know he's keeping his distance. That kiss was more than he wanted, I know because the guilt in his eyes afterward was apparent.

We were all meant to hate her, not want to sit and listen to her painful recollections of a monster she grew up with. But we do. None of us can deny it because it's clear as fucking day.

By the time I'm pushing open the door to her cell, I'm wound up tight. A coiled spring. She's sitting on the bed, still in a pair of panties and a T-shirt. It's been a few days since I saw her, and even though we've not allowed her to shower, she's still breathtakingly beautiful.

"Come," I order, keeping my voice calm, but my insides are twisted with need.

"Where are you taking me?" Even in her predicament, she's strong, fiery. I want to smile at her, but I don't. If I do, she'll take it the wrong way, she'll think I'm being nice. I'm not.

"If you don't want to leave this room, so be it. But I'm not going to repeat myself." I turn and leave her behind. Her footsteps patter behind me and I smile as I lead the way upstairs to the main section of the house.

In the kitchen, I glance at her from over my

shoulder, taking in the dirty girl. Fuck, she is stunning. It's frustrating. I lead her up to the first floor, which houses a couple of guest rooms, along with a bathroom. I shove open the door and gesture for her to enter.

"What is going on?" Her wariness isn't unfounded. She should be scared. She should be very fucking scared. When we hated her, she was safer. Now, the thoughts running through my mind about her are far more volatile.

"Clean yourself up, I'll bring you clothes to wear."

"And then what?'

"You ask too many fucking questions, little mouse," I tell her, pinning her with a heated glare. I can't deal with being so close to her. She's filthy, but I want nothing more than to rip the stupid T-shirt from her body and explore every inch of pale flesh.

"Okay," she finally mumbles and enters the bathroom. I shut the door and lean against it. My head dropping back against the wood. The shower turns on, and I listen for the glass door to slide closed. Once it does, I move away and hunt down something for her to wear. Because if one thing is clear, she cannot walk around our house with a pair of panties on and nothing else.

When I return to the bathroom, I shove open the door only to find her wrapped in a towel. Her skin glistens with water droplets, and her hair hangs in a long, sleek curtain. The blonde seems to be even whiter, making her look like a goddamned angel.

"Found these for you," I hand her a pair of sweatpants and a loose fitting tee. It will cover up her body and keep us focused on the task at hand—to not kill her or fuck her. To get information out of her. We need to learn more about the connections her father has. Since Falcon is on the case, digging into the Bratva, I have a feeling we're still going to need insider info.

"Thank you," Lucille says quietly. "I didn't expect you to be nice to me. I understand your anger," she tells me which seems to only heat my blood with fury.

"You understand nothing," I tell her. "You were not targeted by a monster who stole from you."

"Tell me what he did to each of you, please?" Her plea almost has me breaking down. But I'm stronger and her begging steels my resolve. I can't allow myself to feel anything more than anger. Because if I do, I'm afraid I'll never stop. It can't happen.

"You'll find out soon enough. Get dressed," I tell her before shutting the door so she can't ask me anything more. She's alluring. There's something about her which has monsters craving her, monsters like us. Falcon wants her, and Hawk has made it clear he does too. My own feelings of desire are burning through me like a wildfire.

It's time she pays her dues. When the door opens, she's dressed, and her hair is slowly drying which turns the white to a soft golden color. I turn and head down the hall, her footsteps behind me the only clue she's following. I take her into the kitchen.

"It's almost lunch time, we'll want something to eat. Help yourself to anything," I tell her. "But remember, you're here to do as we say."

"And if I don't?"

I spin on my heel and lean into her. She's tiny, which has me looming over her like a shadow. But she doesn't cower, she merely arches a brow at me which makes my dick hard. Her fire is a turn on, and now she's all fresh and smelling like a goddamned snack, I want to devour her.

"Stop asking questions," I tell her firmly. Lifting my hand, I run my knuckles over her cheek, the soft skin making my blood boil. "And you won't get hurt. But if you continue to fight back," I whisper, keeping my voice low and threatening, "we will be forced to use violence to make you submit."

"I could run," she tells me adamantly.

I laugh out loud. The thought of her even trying to get out of this house, and off the property is not a worry I have. There is no way she'll make it to the property line, let alone beyond.

"I'd like to see you try," I inform her, tipping my

head to the side as I regard the feisty little mouse. "Because if you haven't garnered this from us yet, we love the chase."

Lucille steps back from me, putting space between us and moves around the counter to the fridge. She doesn't respond, and I doubt she will. What she does need to do is accept her place in this house. For now, she's nothing more than a maid, someone to do things for us. Anything we ask of her.

I leave her be and head to Falcon's office. I find him leaning back in his seat, on a call. Settling into the armchair opposite his desk, I wait until he hangs up.

"That was Drake," he tells me. "He's figured out the connection to the Bratva. Apparently, Mahoney got involved with them about twenty years ago, before Lucille was born. Between us, we've nailed it down to the fact her father had promised the Pakhan his daughter's hand in marriage."

"So it was while his wife was pregnant?"

Falcon nods. "It seems so. But then he went back on his word when Lucille was born. This meant he pissed off one of the most dangerous men in the world. It's when he went to the Cartel for protection, leaving the Bratva angry and out for revenge."

"But it still doesn't explain Lucille's involvement in the—"

"This bastard who runs the Cartel who

Mahoney was working for was into trafficking. He was making bank on it. Any age welcome. The deal was Mahoney gets these kids, sends them off to Mexico, and his daughter is kept safe from harm."

"So how are they keeping an eye on her when she's here?" I ask, confusion still blurring the edges of my focus.

Falcon leans forward and says, "They're not, because the men were called off when Mahoney was incarcerated."

"But what about the rumors the Bratva were going to bust him out?"

"New deal," Falcon announces with a grin of pure satisfaction. He's always enjoyed puzzles, this is no different. Figuring out what is going on in a job gets him excited. "Mahoney contacted them, begged forgiveness, and told them he'll bring his daughter in."

It all clicks into place. "Because she testified against her father in court." Falcon nods. Of course the man is angry. His only child made sure he was sent to prison. "That means he'll come after her the moment he's out."

"Exactly, and I have a feeling he knows she's in England. There's no way he won't know. He'll be on a private plane heading this way the moment he steps foot out of prison. I'm not sure how they plan to break him out, but it will be worldwide news."

"Then we need to keep tabs on him. I don't want her finding out about this," I inform Falcon. "If she's aware of his plan, she'll try to run and it will only put her in more danger."

"Are you worried about her now?" Falcon's brow arches as he regards me. I've been too open about my concern for her. I should have known one of my best friends will notice it. Generally I'm good at keeping my emotions in cheek, but the thought of Lucille' being sold off to some bastard doesn't sit well with me. I realize it's because I want to be the one to make her cry, I want to hurt her.

"Don't read into shit." I push to my feet, but I can feel Falcon's gaze boring into me. When I look up, he's regarding me with a knowing smirk. "Don't."

"I'm not doing anything, brother," he tells me with a chuckle. "I mean, don't get me wrong, it would be fun if we all three enjoyed the beauty. Can you picture it right now?" he says as he stands, grabbing his crotch. The fucker knows how to get to me. "She could take us both, all three for that matter. Her tight body filled with three cocks making her scream."

"You're a dick," I bite out while shaking my head. But I don't deny the image in my mind is alluring. It has my own cock twitching with need. She'd be so tight, so warm. It's been too long since I've been inside a woman.

"But you love it," Falcon throws back as he rounds the desk and follows me out of his office. His warmth against my back as he leans in to whisper in my ear, "I'm horny, shall we play with our toy?"

This has me chuckling. Bastard really knows how to get to me. There are times Falcon can diffuse a situation with his humor. There is a light-hearted spark to him which sparks calm in both me and Hawk. But even so, Falcon can be deadly when he needs to be. It's what makes him special.

We make our way to the kitchen to find it empty. My stomach sinks the moment I don't see her, and my gaze flicks to the back door which is still shut. If she did escape, she closed it behind her. But the perimeter alarms haven't sounded, so she can't be outside.

"Where is she?"

I shake my head. "Don't know." I turn and head for the living room, while Falcon is hot on my trail. I come to a stop when I see standing in front of the large flat screen is our girl. The two words burn a hole right into my gut, but I shake it off because right now is not the time to be considering what it could mean.

The news on screen is the only thing my focus should be on.

My stomach churns with knowing as I listen to the report.

Fifteen
LUCILLE

I HEARD THEM TALKING AND NOW I'M STANDING IN their living room in shock. I should never have eavesdropped on Falcon and Crow, but when I went to ask them about lunch, I stopped short when I heard my father's name. He's going to get out, there is no doubt about it, but the fact he's going to come for me has unease coiling in my stomach.

I raced into the lounge to turn on the news, and now, as I stare at the screen, my chest tightens with panic.

A jailbreak at the Molehill Penitentiary.

My heart stops. My lungs struggle with air as I stare at the reporter outside the prison. High walls, barbed wire, and cameras in every corner, and yet, three men have escaped. Three. As their names pop up on the screen, the mug I'd been holding falls from my hand.

It crashes to the floor, but I don't hear it. I only hear my father's name repeating over and over again. *Lionel Mahoney.* It's no longer my name, I changed it legally years ago. But I can't stop the panic swimming in my eyes which causes my vision to blur.

He's out.

He's free.

The photo of him appears on the television makes bile rise up my throat, burning its trail to my mouth where I force myself to swallow back the fear.

I can't drag my gaze away from the screen. There's evil in the man. He's my father, but there has been a sinister darkness which has followed him around like a shadow. Deep down, I think it's inside me.

I've fought for so long to ignore it. To focus on the good I can do in the world, but as I look at my dad, the man who gave me life, I know whatever is broken in him, is shattered in me. My mother did her best. She thought leaving the country would give me a fresh start, a new perspective, and ninety percent of the time, I am fine.

But it's the other ten percent I can't account for. It's what scares me. Perhaps it happened the day he hurt me. I recall the scar running along my spine, the phantom pain tingling as I think about that night. The sleek blade sliced through me caused a sting of agony which tore my attention from the boys for a second.

I lost control and cost the boys their lives.

That day, I saw the devil in the form of my dad.

"Fuck," Crow's voice cuts through the darkness swimming in my vision. I can't look at him because I know what I'll see—rage. I don't blame him, I feel it too. Deep down in my core, I realize my life is about to change once more.

When I glance over to the two men beside me, I take in their expressions filled with knowing. We're aware of what's about to come; my father will seek me out, and he'll bring along the evil had haunted me for years.

The television still replaying the latest news, and it's Falcon who takes two long strides over to where I'm standing and flicks off the screen. The silence envelops us then is like a heavy weight, slamming down on me.

But I fight the urge to run screaming from their immaculate home. Even if I did run, there is nowhere to go. Strangely, I'm safer here with these men than I am out there. They may hate me, but they'll kill my father before he touches me. I'm certain. The look in Falcon's eyes steals my breath.

"You're not leaving this house," he tells me

adamantly. I wait for Crow to dissuade him, to tell him I'm nothing more than a hinderance, but I'm shocked when he's silent. I glance over Falcon's shoulder to find those silver eyes on me. His hair is messy, the black curls hanging down into his eyes.

"I want to hate you," he tells me then. "But I also want to fuck you so hard you never forget my dick was inside you." Crow's admission has my cheeks warming and I'm pretty sure they're bright red.

I never expected him to say something like that before. The hate part of it, yes, but not the rest. "I'm not afraid of you," I tell him before flicking my gaze toward Falcon. They're both watching me as if I were a flight risk.

Crow takes slow steps toward me before he stops inches from my face. Falcon's to my left, while Crow stands to my right. The corner of his mouth tilts upward, a smirk of anger and pure rage turns his expression hard.

"Don't for one second think I won't hurt you," he says. "Because even though I want to fuck you, I still want to see you cry."

"I'm still not afraid of you," I bite out, causing Falcon to chuckle as I turn to face Crow straight on. We're face to face, his body tall, broad, looming over mine as if I were nothing more than a rag doll he can throw over his shoulder. He doesn't think twice as he takes my wrists in his hands and shoves them behind my back.

Falcon takes over, holding me with one hand, bound so I can't fight the man before me. Crow pulls out his knife, and it's then I notice it's carved. The sleek silver matches his eyes, and the flying crow adorning the shimmering metal blinks at me in the light.

Like he did before in his office, he slices the material covering me. The soft cotton falls open, baring my breasts to him. "I've wanted to do this for so long," he murmurs, running the sharp tip along my collarbone, down between my cleavage, until he reaches my navel. "You know if I were to push, hard, you'd be dead within in a, hour. Maybe less."

I don't move. I don't even blink. My breaths are halted as I wait for the pain, but it never comes. He runs the weapon lower, until the sweatpants that were hugging my hips fall to the ground, along with my panties. Now, I'm standing in front of my captor bared for his hungry, rage-filled gaze.

"Drink this," Falcon tells me as he hands me the tumbler.

With shaking hands, I grasp the expensive crystal and bring it to my lips. The stench of alcohol is eye-watering, but I ignore it and close my eyes. I swallow back the strong liquid and set the glass down on the table.

"I don't know what to do," I tell them as my

gaze flicks between the two men. "I can't do this. I can't stay here. There's no way—"

"You're not going anywhere," Falcon repeats his earlier words. Without warning, he claims my lips without asking permission. I find I don't care. The warmth at my back tells me Crow is behind me. His hands trail along my arms from shoulder to wrist, and then, he tugs me back until my ass is right up against his crotch. The hardness nestles on my ass makes me gasp into Falcon's mouth and he enjoys the sounds.

I can feel eyes on me. Burning through me. When I open my eyes, pulling away from Falcon, I find Hawk, staring at us. He's worried. He should be. I'm caught between the most dangerous men I've met in a long time, and they want my blood. But it's not them I fear. It's my father.

"Join us," I call to Hawk, who's stare turns venomous. He spins on his heel and walks out, leaving us standing in the living room. Crow's hand snakes around my waist, and teases its way down to my core. He doesn't care his friend is angry, instead, he dips his finger between the lips of my pussy finding me wet.

"You like it. Don't you, little mouse?" Crow whispers in my ear, Falcon's eyes burn as he watches. I want to ask about Hawk, but when another finger slips inside me, I lose all focus. My head drops back into Crow's shoulder and my eyes roll back in my head. Pleasure zings through every nerve in my body.

"W-what about—"

"He'll be back," Falcon whispers along my neck. "Now, you should be focused on us," he tells me, and I can feel his lips slip into a smile along my skin which sends heat coursing through me.

Crow's fingers dip deeper, they spread me open, stretching me, and he inserts a third digit. The wet sounds of my arousal echo around us as I whimper at the intrusion. I can't think about anything else right now. It's only him, them, both men cocooning me in warmth.

"Such a good fucking slut for us," Crow hisses as he leans in and captures my lower lip between his teeth. He bites down hard, earning himself a moan of pure ecstasy.

This is what I need. What I crave.

I haven't allowed myself to feel anything in so long. When Crow reaches for my nipple, and pinches it, twisting the peaked bud, I cry out his name. My body convulses around his fingers, pulsing, drenching him until I hear a dark chuckle.

"Little slut, like it's deep," he murmurs before capturing my nipple in his mouth and sucking on it so hard, pain shoots through me, zapping me between my thighs.

"Think you can handle another one?" Falcon teases, his hot breath in my ear sending shivers down my spine.

"Yes," I hiss, the need to be fucked savagely taking a hold of me. Seconds later, I'm lifted by Falcon, my body weighing nothing in his strong hold. His hands under my thighs, spreading me open. It's Crow who unzips his jeans. His cock juts out toward me, the tip weeping with arousal. Thick, hard, and beautiful. He grips himself in one fist before slapping my clit with the wet head of his dick.

I look down at where we're going to connect, and the sight of him already painting me with his wetness makes me pulse with need. He lines himself with my entrance, and without warning, he ruts against me, his cock hitting me deep. The bite pain of him stretching me sends bliss shooting through my veins.

I feel as if I'm drunk. Falcon holds me with no effort as his best friend fucks me. Their bodies are hot, scorching me, enveloping me in desire as Falcon's lips find my neck, and he sucks the flesh hard, until I'm moaning out his name.

Both names fall from my lips in quick succession as euphoria takes over and I can no longer form a coherent sentence. Crow cups my breasts in his hands, squeezing, mauling them as if he wants me to cry.

Agonizing lust burns me from the inside out. The thickness of his dick hits the entrance of my womb, and I can't help but beg for more. This is what I want, what I always seek. I don't want gentle love-making. My body craves the animalistic fucking, it's what I need. And these men give it to me.

"Come on my cock," Crow orders, his voice rough with desire. His fingers dig into the flesh of my tits, and I know he's leaving bruises. He's marking me. He's the first of the three to have me, and he wants me to remember him. "Come hard on my dick, little slut," he commands once more, and I can't hold back my bliss.

I choke out his name as his one hand wraps around my neck, squeezing tight, until I can't feel my lungs work. My lips part, my eyes roll back and I see sparks behind the lids. Nothing can keep me from an orgasm as I drench him.

My thighs shake, trembling on either side of this monster who's made me come harder than anyone ever has. My focus is lost. I can't think straight. My toes curl, and I'm clawing at Crow, but all I hear are the sounds of his chuckle.

Time passes.

My body is slowly lowered and I stand on wobbly legs. The wetness of his seed trickles down my thighs, but I don't care. It's no use trying to cover myself in front of these men. They've seen it all.

When I finally open my eyes, I notice Hawk at the doorway, his cock in hand, and his release coating his fingers. I know no matter how much he *wants* to hate me, he also wants to fuck me.

Sixteen
FALCON

JESUS FUCKING CHRIST.

I can honestly say I've never been so goddamned hard before. Watching them fuck, seeing her body take Crow's dick, and the sounds she made did something feral to me. It turned me rabid with need to taste her.

I didn't expect this woman to change our outlook on the plan, the idea we had was to end her, and her father. But now, Crow has claimed her and there is nothing she can do about it. Hawk watches from the sidelines.

Crow looks over at me, his hands still on Lucille. Everything has changed. I knew he wouldn't be able to ignore his feelings for her. I've known Crow most of my life, and he isn't someone who can stop himself when he wants something.

He has craved this woman since his gaze first landed on her. He turns her toward me, her eyes wide as she takes me in. The pupils still dilated from her earlier orgasm.

"Do you want to watch us, little mouse?" Crow whispers in her ear. Hawk moves closer, unable to stop himself. We've all been caught in this girl's trap. She's a lure, a siren, edging us close to our demise, and it seems we're happily jumping to our death.

Lucille nods, but her eyes hold mine. It's almost as if she's asking my permission to say yes. I offer a small smile, enough to give her what she needs.

"Yes." Her whisper is a prayer, a plea. She's needy, still after what we've given her. A hungry little slut. I love it.

I reach for my top, tugging the material over my head. When it falls to the floor, I undo my belt with a clang, and then, the hiss of my zipper echoes around us. In my peripheral, I can see Hawk closing the distance.

When I shove my jeans to the floor, my cock tents my boxers. I'm so hard, it's painful. I'm hungry for anyone to put their mouth on me. I don't care who it is. Crow, Hawk, even our sweet little siren.

She stares at me, and when I grip my dick in my boxers, a hiss of pure pleasure escapes my lips. Crow takes Lucille's hand, and leads her over to the sofa, where they both drop down to their knees in front of the large cushions. I know what he wants, so I follow suit, settling on the dark material seating and allowing him to lead her to tug at my boxers. Once they hit the floor, Crow leans in and laps at my dick, sending warmth shooting through my veins.

Lucille's gaze widens. She watches, enraptured by Crow's lips on my dick. They wrap around the weeping tip, and he sucks me in deep. The tightness of his throat pulsing around me, sending waves of pleasure through every inch of me.

When he pops his mouth off, he glances over to Lucille who's only now noticed the bar on the underside of my dick. Her mouth opens, then closes.

"Stick your tongue out for me, darling?" I coo, waiting for her to obey. When she does, Crow helps her forward, and I slap her tongue with my dick a few times. The warmth of her wet tongue against the hardness of my dick makes every nerve in my body come alive. As if I've been electrocuted.

"Suck his cock with me," Crow tells her, and they move in sync. Pouting their lips, they slide up and down my shaft, causing my eyes to roll back in my head. When I feel hands on me, I snap my gaze open to find Hawk leaning in to press his lips to mine. The wetness of the two mouths, along with Hawk's tongue in my mouth is pushing ever so close to the edge.

The flavor of his kiss is tinged with whiskey. His tongue duels with mine, fighting for more, for dominance, but I don't let him have it. He needs to calm down. His hands trail down my chest, right down to where the two mouths are gifting me immense pleasure.

I don't know how we're going to get through this, how Lucille is going to feel with all of us sharing, but when I reach for her and pull her onto the couch, she offers me a smile. There's a shyness to her. Earlier, she'd lost herself in the need, but now she seems more focused on the fact there are three of us, and one of her.

I pull her closer, making her straddle me. Her wet heat still sticky from having Crow's release trickling from her entrance. "My turn," I tell her as I grip my dick and position it at her pussy. She's warm and slick as I slip inside her. Slow, steady, and inch by inch, she takes me.

Crow stands behind her, his hands trailing over her smooth skin. Her back arches and he takes it as his cue. He kneels between my thighs, his hands spreading her ass, and when Lucille gasps in shock, I know where his talented tongue is.

"Crow—" Her gasp is cut off when she winces, and leans forward, as if trying to get away from him. But there's nowhere to run. Not now, not ever. Crow is still set on killing her, but I don't see it happening.

"This little hole needs to be broken in," Crow rumbles as he rises to full height. From my vantage point, I can't deny the sight of him naked behind her is exquisite.

"Starting the party without me?" he asks, his eyes on mine. He doesn't look at her, at Lucille, but he can't deny she's attractive. He reaches us and pulls the T-shirt from his body. The material falls to the floor in a soft whoosh, and the blood is now obvious.

"What—" Lucille's words are cut off when Hawk grabs a ball gag, and waves it in front of her face.

"You need to be quiet," he tells her. "Or I will be forced to hurt you." I expect her to fight him or argue, but she doesn't. Hawk is gentle when he ties the leather strap around her head. The little red ball looks pretty between those fat lips as they shimmer with saliva.

"Such a pretty slut," Crow says as he presses his mouth against her cheek. "Today, you'll learn exactly what we want from you," he informs her in a whisper veiled with darkness.

Hawk takes the rear, as Crow moves out of the way. A soft buzzing comes from Hawk's hand, and I know he's probably hidden toys in the pocket of his jeans. A small, powerful vibrator appears in his hand. He holds it beside Lucille's face, and grins when she tries to scoot away.

"Time to play." He trails the toy over her shoulder as goose bumps rise in its wake. Crow leans in beside me, stealing my lips in a kiss, while Lucille's tight cunt squeezes my dick. The vibrator taunts her nipples, causing her to whimper into the ball gag, and the wetness of her spit drips from her chin.

The smell of sex hangs in the air, and by the time Hawk reaches her ass, the gentle vibrations reach all the way to my balls, sending jolts of pleasure through me. I take Crow's dick in my hand and stroke it. Hawk moves closer, the toy sending pleasurable tingles up my spine and then, it's gone.

His hand reaches for Lucille's throat, gripping the column to pull her backward before Crow moves to my mouth, and I take his thick cock between my lips. I spy out of the corner of my eye, Lucille watching in awe as I suck my best friend deep.

Hawk moves closer to her, and I watch from the corner of my eye as he bites down on her earlobe, causing her to whimper into the gag. Her cunt grips me each time his teeth sinks into the flesh.

"Such a pretty, needy slut for us," Hawk grits through clenched teeth as he reaches around to cup her tits. His fingers twist her pert little nipples as Crow grips his dick, pulling it from my mouth. He smirks as he turns, slapping the thick shaft against her face. Lucille is nothing more than a ball of bliss, lost in the darkness with us. My cock jolts when Hawk tilts his head, while pinching her nipples, he allows his teeth to graze along Crow's hard, thick shaft.

"Fuck," Crow bites out, his fist tightening around his dick. Suddenly, Hawk chuckles and Lucille's eyes widen. "Take it little slut," Crow murmurs when he leans in to lap at the emotion trickling from her eyes. "Take his dick in your pert little ass," he tells her and soon enough, my dick is being massaged by Hawk's. Lucille's body trembles, shakes, and tightens as he enters her.

Crow's deep growl steals my attention as he whips off the gag and replaces it with his cock. Every inch of Lucille is now ours, and there is no longer any doubt in my mind she is ours.

Claimed. Owned. Completely and utterly destroyed.

It's beautiful. Watching her take us, watching her revel in the adoration we offer, no matter how dark and filthy it is, makes me want so much more from her. I want to take and take until there's nothing left. I've hungered for someone who is able to enjoy us, who can lose herself in our sordid needs, and it seems our Goldilocks can.

She's pinned between three monstrous men, and she's not afraid. Instead, she's turned us into rabid bears, hungry to devour. I want to lick and taste every inch of her, every fucking day.

We move in sync.

Our bodies are ruled by desire.

The darkness in Lucille's shimmering eyes dances like devils on a fire. She regards me as I lift my hips, while Hawk fucks her mercilessly. Every thrust expels a whimper from her plump lips.

Crow takes her ruthlessly. The sound of her throat working to swallow his cock doesn't stop my own from throbbing. Rough force is an aphrodisiac, and each time he fills her mouth, her cunt tightens, pulsing around my dick.

The sound of sex is a debauched symphony filling my senses as if I were inhaling intoxicating fumes. As if I were high on the destruction of this beautiful woman. I fucking love it.

I grip her hips, while Hawk cups her tits. Our hands tease and taunt, and the closer I get to the edge, I know we're never going to let her go. Crow's hand wraps around Lucille's throat, and he squeezes, while his dick is buried deep in her esophagus. Her eyes widen, and he smiles down at her.

I watch as he leans in and allows his saliva to dribble from his tongue into her mouth as she tries to pull in air. The sight is so erotic, I dig my fingers into her hips, the soft flesh giving way, and I thrust one last time, my release filling her, coating her inside, making sure my mark is there.

"Fuck," Hawk grunts, and his head drops back, pleasure painted across his features as he finds bliss, while Crow sucks Lucille's tongue into his mouth.

He murmurs against her lips, "Our little slut." He grins manically as she fights for breath, her cunt choking the life out of my now softening dick.

I can't help smiling as I reach for her hardened little nub, and I pinch her clit until she's mewling, the sound nothing more than a croak as she tries to call out one of our names. It could be a prayer, or it could be a cry for mercy, but Crow doesn't know about leniency.

He moves into her mouth, and grunts before his own release paints her tongue, then her cheeks. "Such a pretty, dirty, little girl."

When he moves away, I cup her face in my hands and pull her in, tugging her closer until she's inches from me. With slow, gentle strokes, I lap at the salty release, and we share it in a kiss made of lust and desire. Passion ignites between us, and Hawk's two fingers, dripping with his own cum is offered to us like the goddamned communion.

Lucille takes it without thinking, and I watch as she sucks both digits clean, before she tangles her tongue with mine, and we share the sticky, salty fluid.

I've never come across a woman so open to

filth. To the darkness. I have never met a woman who enjoys the scenes we do, but she does. As her cunt drips down my thighs, I can't help but enjoy the warmth of the three bodies around me.

This may have been our first foray into a foursome, but it certainly won't be the last.

Seventeen

LUCILLE

THE GUYS HAVE BEEN WORKING, AND I'VE BEEN HOLED up in the guest bedroom. I'm no longer locked in a basement, which feels good. After our intimate evening, having them both practically worship me, I've been on edge. You don't go from hate to lust so quickly. Granted, a hate fuck is always good. But with all three of them being busy with trying to find my father and his associates, I've been left to my own devices.

But boredom has set in. There is only so much reality television you can watch before you go stir crazy. I'm not allowed to leave the house. I don't mind, because if Dad does find me, I don't want to be vulnerable. That will only end up with me dead or sold off to some Bratva leader.

I still haven't told them what had happened. It's one thing which has been bothering me. I know if I confessed about my past, they would look at me differently. I don't want to see the pity in their eyes.

I survived and I'm stronger for it. Most of those nights I've locked away in my mind. It's safe in a box where it can't hurt me. But the moment the lock is picked, I'm going to break down. Secrets can only be hidden for so long, and when they break free, there's no stopping it.

I move through the house silently. There isn't a noise coming from anywhere. I find myself in Crow's bedroom, which is all black. It fits him. The darkness he exudes is so obvious in the furnishings. The sleek king sized bed on a platform of charcoal metal. I flick a switch by his bedside, and the floor under the bed illuminates with a deep blue. The headboard and nightstands are made of the same dark gray material.

The sheets are black along with the pillowcases. A floor to ceiling window overlooks darkness. The moon is hidden by the clouds, so the rest of the room is in shadows. The walls are painted in black, but the carpet is pure white. Cabinets with drawers sit opposite the bed, with a flat screen attached to the wall above.

I move through the space, inhaling his scent of cedar and cinnamon. It's masculine, and yet, calming. In his walk in closet, I run my fingertips over the material of his suits, shirts, and his workout clothes.

I haven't seen a gym here yet, but I'm certain there's one. The house is so big. I haven't had a chance to explore every room yet. Back in the bedroom, I turn left and head for the attached bathroom. The color scheme flows from room to room, and the dark tiles make the space seem warmer, cozier.

A large shower sits in the corner, while a black porcelain bathtub is perched on a tiled platform which is beside a window. I can imagine lying in there, enjoying a bubble bath while taking in the view. Two mirrors sit above the two basins, while the black cabinets hide underneath. I pull open the doors as curiosity takes a hold of me.

Nothing but some toiletries, and towels.

I shouldn't snoop, but learning about one of the men who have held me captive is essential. At first, I wanted so badly to escape, to run for my life, but my feelings have changed somewhat.

What they did is wrong, but I find myself intrigued by them. When they fucked me, when they claimed me, I was lost in euphoria. I had never met a man who could offer me what I needed. My body craves what they can give. But they're still dangerous.

There's no telling what they'll do to me once

they get to my father. The end game was always to kill me, I have no doubt. The hate they hold is not unwarranted, I get it, but I'd also like to live.

I move back into the bedroom, before taking one last long look around. When I shut the door behind me, I turn to the right and find the next room. Shoving open the door, I note with ease it's Falcon's space.

One wall is filled with books. From floor to ceiling. He has a rolling ladder which allows him access to the top shelves. His room is furnished in browns, soft, gentle colors, along with olive green which offers warmth. It's like walking into the log cabin in the middle of winter, with a fire roaring in the background.

His bed is decked in a dark brown comforter, the pillows a similar green to his eyes. There is a door to the left of the bed which leads onto a balcony, but I don't open it. It's cold enough in the house.

When I find his closet, I notice it has the same color scheme as Crow's, all blacks, dark grays, and only a handful of crisp white shirts. Everything else is dark.

I feel like Goldilocks, in the home of the three bears as I explore each of their bedrooms. I'm not sure I want to see Hawk's room. I have a feeling if I'm caught in there, I'll be shut back down in the basement.

He hasn't accepted me into the home. Not like the other two have. Their anger is still apparent; however it's not completely focused on me. They're now solely fixated on finding my father.

In saying that, I think I'll refrain from looking for Hawk's bedroom. Perhaps in a few weeks, if I'm still here, and alive, I'll find the courage to seek it out. I sit down on Falcon's bed, the scent of his cologne overwhelms me. A woodsy fragrance which reminds me of the forest after an evening of rain. The fresh, excitement of a new day.

I smile to myself when I think of Falcon. I know he's a killer, but I feel safe around him. More so than the other two. Crow is addicted to the kill, to the darkness. He'll devour me whole with a smile on his face.

With a quick glance at the time, I note it's almost two in the morning, and exhaustion plagues me. I lean back on the mattress and rest my head on the pillow. I know I should go to my own room, but I want to settle here for a little while.

* * *

"Wake, wakey, Goldilocks," Falcon's amused tone jolts me. My gaze snaps open to find him grinning down at me. "If I didn't know any better, I would think you wanted me to eat you," he tells me with a chuckle.

My cheeks heat in embarrassment. I must have

been more tired than I thought. I figured I'd have a rest, but not fall asleep and not wake up.

"I didn't know when you guys were coming home," I tell him. My voice is scratchy, my head is throbbing, and I'm ready to fall asleep again. It's still dark out, so it can't have hit sunrise yet.

"I'm tired, so either you stay there and sleep beside me, or you leave now," he says then, "Either way, you have five seconds before I slide into bed behind you." When I don't move, he merely shakes his head and smiles. His warm body nestles behind mine, and he wraps an arm around my waist. "We'll talk in the morning."

For a long while, I can't fall back asleep. All I can think of is Falcon holding me. It's strange my once kidnapper is now cuddling me in bed. But the warmth of him soon sends me back to sleep.

Pleasure zips down my spine, and my legs tremble when my groggy brain catches up. The sun is streaming through the window. My eyes open and I glance down to find Falcon between my thighs. His hands spreading me open, and his tongue lashing my pussy sending waves of bliss through me.

I open my mouth to speak, but he dips a finger inside me, causing me to forget every thought in my mind. With Falcon's ministrations, I'm lost to the pleasure he's bestowing on my body, and I don't notice the other man enter the room.

Crow settles on the mattress beside me, surprising me when he trails his fingers over my nipples. One at a time, he teases them until they're hardened peaks. The dark, curly hair I've come to love falls into his eyes, making the silver nothing more than slivers of metal.

"Looks like someone is having an early breakfast," he murmurs along my lips, glancing down at Falcon who laughs against my wetness, sending vibrations through my pussy.

"Jealous much?" he taunts Crow who runs his fingers down my body until he reaches my mound. He dips two fingers inside me, rubbing along my front wall causing my hips to buck.

When he pulls both digits away, he brings them to his lips and sucks them clean of my juices. It's hot, so fucking erotic, I nearly lose all control watching him.

"Delicious," Crow remarks, before he moves onto his knees and shoves his boxers down. His cock is hard, jutting toward my mouth, and I take the opportunity to lean forward and run my tongue along the base.

A hiss of pleasure escapes his full lips, and I do it again before wrapping my lips around the tip. His salty flavor bursts on my tongue. He doesn't waste time, his hand grips the back of my head, and he holds me steady, using my mouth as Falcon continues devouring me.

Each moan which vibrates in my throat, I receive another thrust of Crow's hips. But as I'm sure he's about to lose all control, he pulls his cock from my mouth and turns to Falcon.

"Let's have some fun," he says, and the other man nods with a smile. I'm not sure what they're planning, but it's soon obvious when Falcon's shorts hit the ground and he's fisting his pierced dick at my entrance.

Gently, he slips into me, stretching me. The metal against my walls has my pussy pulsing around his length. Falcon leans over me, his mouth brushing along my lips, and I taste myself on his tongue.

A moan vibrates through his chest when Crow enters him. The three of us joined, connected. It's intense. It's beautiful to watch them fucking. There's no gentle love-making, but their emotions are clear. They would die for each other.

Their bodies are impeccable. Toned, chiseled. Defined with dips and peaks I want to run my tongue along. But as Falcon's cock hits me deep, Crow fucks him harder. The movement is perfectly synced, and we all lose ourselves in the sounds of fucking.

I do wish Hawk was here, I wish he'd let go and enjoy himself, but for now, I close my eyes and find my bliss with these two men. Falcon's mouth captures my nipple, while his fingers taunt the other.

My skin is bruised from them groping and grabbing me, but I wouldn't have it any other way. I'm marked by them. I'm owned and claimed, even before I knew what was happening. It's bliss. It's perfect.

I shouldn't enjoy it as much as I do, but these men know how to make me feel. It's as if I'm alive for the first time in my life, and I'm soaring through the clouds when I feel Falcon's cock thicken and pulse as he fills me with his release.

I follow close behind as I cry out, my arousal soaking us both. I feel the jolts of Crow's thrusts as he grunts out is pleasure. Three sweaty bodies, connected by lust, joined by desire, and euphoric in our darkness.

Crow moves first, before Falcon follows suit. He stands, offering his hand which I accept. "Time to clean our dirty girl up," he says with a smile and leads me to the shower. Crow is close behind, and I am not sure why I feel so safe with them, but I do.

I don't know how long it's going to last.

Eighteen
LUCILLE

W E'VE FALLEN INTO A ROUTINE.
But today I want to learn more. I need to see
what they do. Each evening they leave for a job, and
I'm left alone. I want to go with them, and I hope
when I bring it up, I pray they allow me in. If I'm
going to stay here, if I'm going to be one of them,
then I need to know everything there is to know. All
the ugly details.

I'm still wary of them though. They can turn on
me at any time, so I watch my back. But as each day
passes it's another one I learn more about them. As
I walk into Crow's office, I'm nervous. My stomach
is in knots when I find him behind his desk. He's
already dressed for a job they're heading out to
tonight, which means I have to move fast if I want to

go with them.

"Any news?" I settle in the chair opposite his desk.

Crow's silver eyes take me in from head to toe. I'm wearing a pair of black tights, along with my combat boots and a hoodie. I'm dressed for comfort. But if he gives me the go ahead, I have a dress in mind which I can easily change into.

When Falcon said they're buying me clothes, I wasn't sure what to expect, but he allowed me onto his computer, while supervised, but I could choose what I wanted to wear. Crow observed as I excitedly bought what I wanted. Now I have a closet of clothes.

"Not yet, we know he's hiding out in L.A., but the moment he makes a move, we'll hear about it," Crow assures me. "Was there something else on your mind, little mouse?" The dark arch of his brow reminds me he's extremely perceptive. I can't lie to him, and I can't hide anything because Crow notices everything.

"I want to go on a job." It's now or never. There's no point in making up reasons as to why I'm in his office.

"No."

"Why not? I can do what you do, and I could probably do it better."

Crow laughs out loud at me. "Oh really? You can kill a man without blinking and walk away

183

from it without guilt?" I knew they killed people, but I didn't think they did it every night. I wanted to learn more about them. About their work.

"Let me go with you, I can be your arm candy."

This time, he leans back in his chair, elbows resting on the arms of the seat. "What makes you think I need you as arm candy?" His challenge is clear. Those silver eyes shimmer as he regards me with the corner of his mouth tipping upward in a smirk. He's cocky. Arrogant. But I can't deny it turns me on.

"Because if you didn't need me, I wouldn't be here anymore," I throw back, hoping I'm not overstepping. He could so easily pull out his knife and launch it at my head. Then I'll be fucked.

He leans forward, steepling his fingers under his chin. The black curl I've come to enjoy, falls into his left eye. "And what pray tell, makes you think I don't already have a girl on standby?"

My mouth pops open, but I shut it quickly. I didn't think he would be with anyone else. That was my mistake. I should never have assumed I was the only woman in his life. The man is. Greek god, how can he not have a bevy of beauties lining up to escort him to any event he attends.

"I want to know what you do," I respond without answering his question. I don't want him to think I'm jealous. I don't want to admit it to myself either. I shouldn't be. We're nothing more than captor and captive, who enjoy fucking each other. There's nothing more to it, no feelings.

But even as I think it, I know it's a lie because deep down, I'm starting to like them, all of them. Hawk is still cold toward me. Crow is different, he's ice, but there is more to him than meets the eye. I intend on finding out what it is.

"Fine," he finally appeases, and I almost jump out of my seat to hug him. I shouldn't be this excited to watch him kill someone, but the thought of getting out of this house has me anxious. "Let's get one thing straight," Crow says, holding up a finger. "The men you'll be around tonight, they're nothing like us. They're evil. They won't think twice of gutting you like a fish."

I nod, and hope I don't sound afraid when I say, "I get that."

"No," he bites out as he pins me with a glare. "You don't. You think you do because of your dad, but this is the Bratva we're meeting with. They don't know your name, and they won't know it. You'll walk in there as my fucking slave. If you so much as utter a word to me without my requesting you to speak, I'll happily give you to them."

"Okay," I answer. "I'll obey, and I'll do anything you ask of me. Let me go with you. Please?" He doesn't realize I want to see something other than this place. As beautiful as the house is, it's driving me crazy staying indoors all this time.

"Get dressed, we leave in twenty minutes," Crow orders and I'm on my feet in seconds. "Make sure you're dressed to make dicks hard; I need them distracted." His words are commanding, his eyes though are glued to his computer screen. It's as if he isn't affected by me in any way, shape, or form.

But I know he is.

I rush up to my room with a smile on my face. I've gotten what I want, and I'm excited to be able to do this. My father would take me to meetings, parties, and yet, I was always the entertainment. This time, I'll be a guest. A thought hits me, and I wonder if they'll be similar to the parties I attended as a teenager.

Will there be sex shows out in the open, or will they be more private? There is no doubt what kind of men these are. When Crow said I was to be his slave, it's obvious what will be expected of me, I hope he doesn't do what Dad did.

There was never a time I felt at ease after I learned about my father. Home was no longer a place of refuge, but a place of torment. Now I'm with these men, I've finally found a sense of solace.

I can't explain it. I can't deny I'm losing my mind because I should hate them. I should definitely not be wanting to spend more time with them, and certainly not learning about their work.

But as I pull the dress on over my head, and allow it fall along my curves, I know I'm going to be a part of their family. At first I wanted to escape, but now I'm here, lost in their world, I don't want to run anymore.

Slipping on my heels, I twist and turn in the mirror and take in my appearance. Then, I slowly run my fingers through my long, blonde waves. I don't bother with make-up, but I do darken the lines under my eyes, and add a black mascara which makes the gold of my irises pop.

When I'm done, I head downstairs where I find the three men in the living room. Crow is dressed in a black suit, his white shirt is crisp, crease-free, and the bowtie he's wearing is a deep navy blue. The suit itself fits him perfectly, tailored to his stature, making him seem even more imposing than I could ever have imagined.

All three sets of eyes drink me in. The men hold their tumblers, but the drinks in hand are forgotten. Heat blooms on my cheeks, and for a moment, I feel like a teenage girl heading to her prom.

"Is this okay?" I ask, suddenly unsure of myself. It's silly. I'm a strong woman. I've lived on my own for years. I ran from a monster, only to be caught int he clutches of three rabid bears.

"You're wearing that?" Crow's voice is pure

ice. But there is a twisted darkness in his gaze and it makes my body ache for more of his darkness.

"Yes," I tell him with confidence. There is nothing wrong with my dress. It covers what it needs to, but I can only imagine how his thoughts are currently exploding with scenarios because it hits me mid-thigh, and there is some cleavage showing. The back is covered, mostly, so I don't know what the issue is. "What's wrong with it?"

Crow shakes his head as if answering me is far too difficult. "Let's go." He turns on his heel, and as he leaves the room, I notice Falcon chuckling.

"What's the problem?" I ask him, curiosity taking a hold of me. There's no reason for Crow to act like a jealous boyfriend because it's not at all what he is.

"You frustrate him," Falcon tells me as if it makes perfect sense. It doesn't. Not to me anyway. "The men where you're going will enjoy the dress."

"I thought it was the point." I shrug it off which only makes Falcon laugh louder.

"You're far too innocent at times," he says. "Enjoy your evening." He ushers me from the room, and I don't know if I can say for certain I'll enjoy the evening. It's definitely not my idea of a good time. But at least I'll get to see Crow in action. Something tells me it's a sight to be behold.

By the time I reach the sleek black Maserati,

Crow is waiting at the passenger door. I slip into the seat, and he shuts me in before rounding the front. He's serious, more than usual. The scent of him fills the car when he joins me.

When the engine purrs, I can't help but enjoy the powerful sound as we speed down the drive and out the enormous black gates. I haven't seen the area, because when Hawk brought me here, I was unconscious, so being able to look out at the scenery is a welcome distraction from the man beside me.

He doesn't speak for a long while and my stomach twists with anxiety. I'm not sure if he's angry with me or not, but the way he's gripping the steering wheel tells me he may be angry. Or frustrated. Perhaps both.

"So, what is this event we're going to?" I finally ask because I can't take the quiet anymore. It would've probably been easier if the stereo was on, but I can't deal with a man who's stoically silent.

"The men are auctioning off slaves," he tells me which has my stomach dropping to my feet.

"What?"

"It's an auction for women." Crow doesn't look at me, but his expression is severe. "I need to meet with someone who'll be in attendance. We have intel these men will know when your father is going to arrive in the country."

"These are the Bratva connections?"

"They are," he tells me with a nod.

I turn my attention to the window, taking in the darkness which greets me. The sun set hours ago, and now the sky is black, I can't see much of the countryside. We're nowhere near a city, so I wonder where the party is. Perhaps there are homes along the way, but as we speed through the windy streets, I don't see any lights other than the headlamps of the vehicle.

No one passes us as we take the turns far too quickly for my liking, but I don't say anything to Crow. His focus is on the road, and I want to ask more questions, but I don't. The fear of him selling me off takes a hold, and it's the only thing I can think of as we make our way through the darkness.

I thought I was nervous before, but now, I'm downright scared of what the night holds.

Nineteen
CROW

SHE'S NERVOUS. IT EMANATES THROUGH THE SMALL SPACE of the car, twisting around me like a goddamned ribbon of light. I should put her mind at ease, but it's what a nice guy would do. I'm not a nice person. I rather enjoy her unease. It makes me want to rip the fucking dress off her body and show her how owned she is.

I may not be able to voice my desires, but I can certainly show her with actions. She doesn't realize how much I want her. I didn't until Falcon pointed it out. He frustrates me when he tries to *read* into me. I love fucking and I enjoy fucking this girl who seems to have taken over our lives.

Never once did I think I would keep her safe. That I would want to keep her safe, but I do. Perhaps

191

it's because she is as innocent as we were, like the kids her father stole, her father abused. Those were the children who did nothing to deserve what they got. But I'll ensure her dad gets exactly what he deserves.

The thought of finally ending him is the only reason I'm going to this party tonight. The men who will be in attendance are vile creatures. They all deserve to die. If I wasn't outnumbered, even with my brothers, I would have taken them all out. But there are times where you need to turn the other cheek. Tonight is one of those.

The time will come where they will all pay for their sins.

I may not be innocent in everything I do, but there are limits. I have morals. Even if some may think I don't.

"So," Lucille starts, her voice breaking with nervous energy. "This auction," she says. "It's all women?"

"Virgins," I throw out, ensuring she calms the fuck down. I would have loved to have had her nervous all night, but I need her focused on the task at hand.

"Oh." The soft whisper she breathes does things to me and I have to shift in my seat, my hand ensuring my bulge isn't obvious. "Do you attend these often?"

"Do I look like I need to pay for some tight pussy?" I grit, casting a glance toward her. The way her cheeks flush at my question has my desire only heating my blood more than before.

"No, I mean, I just meant—"

"If a job calls for something, I do it," I explain. "It's the reason I do this. I seek out those who deserve to be killed. I don't do it on a whim. The men we come across are evil. They will do anything they want because they have the money to pay for it. I don't believe a woman should be bought or sold. But I do enjoy a woman to obey when it comes to fucking."

Her questioning gaze turns to me. The heat of it is scorching. Usually, I would hate it, a woman staring at me, but I like her eyes on me. "Is that why you wanted me to work for you?"

I ponder her question. "No. You were meant to be nothing more than revenge on your father. I wanted him to watch as I sliced you open, as you bled out. I wanted him to feel the pain we felt when we lost our siblings."

I glance over to find her mouth popped open and I can't deny, it's beautiful, causing me to think about how my cock would slide along her tongue.

"Don't be shocked," I say, "I told you I enjoy violence, and the blade is my weapon of choice. Usually, I'll have a gun for jobs, but if I had to choose,

193

the agony a slice of metal brings to my victims is far more satisfying."

"Wow," Lucille breathes. "I don't know what to say." She turns her attention away from me, and I want nothing more than to grab her and turn her attention back to me. But I don't. It's not too far now until we reach the house. As much as I didn't want her with me, I knew she had to see what these bastards do. These are the men who are well-known associates of the men her father works for. The same assholes who broke him out of prison. They're the reason she's in danger.

"When we get to the party, you will have to stay silent. Don't speak until I allow you to. If you do, it will put you in danger. If I order you to do something, you do it. I won 't think twice about letting them take you, so do not disobey me."

"I'm not afraid of you, Crow. Also, I'm not going to fuck this up," she bites out. The annoyance in her tone is clear. She's fiery. It's what keeps me wanting to taunt her. The angrier she gets, the more I prod.

"Good," is all I offer before I pull into the driveway of the property. The gates slide open, the heavy metal silently moving offering us entrance. I drive up to the circular drive and stop in front of the enormous double doors.

A valet steps up to my door, waiting for me to give over my keys. Exiting the vehicle, I throw the fob over to him before I make my way around to Lucille's door. I open it and offer her a hand. It's all about appearances and I can't show them we're more familiar than they expect.

Most times, these parties mean the women are nothing more than possessions. If I show any emotion toward her, they'll know something isn't right. If it happens, we'll both be killed. I know my contact is here, but he can't keep us safe since he's undercover, so I have to behave.

"Remember what I said," I whisper as I grip the back of her neck and lead her up to the entrance. There are already guests inside when we enter. Waiters with champagne swan through the crowds, and I grab two flutes, handing one to Lucille. "Drink this," I tell her. The alcohol will calm her nerves. I can't have her tense beside me. She needs to calm the fuck down.

As we move closer to the main room, I find it's filled with guests. I take in the faces, memorizing the expressions. Beside me, Lucille stands anxious, but with every sip of her drink, she seems to lean closer to me. The heat of her is intoxicating, more than the desire coursing through me.

"Who are these people?" Her whisper feathers along my jaw as she looks up at me. The softness of her voice makes me want to take her away. But I can't walk away from her, from this party because there is a job to do.

Music trickles through the speakers, filling the room in a hum of bass and melodies. I wrap my arm around her waist and feel the tension from her ease up. My fingers grip the material of her dress. I'm tempted to rip it off, but I lead her deeper between the men.

Eyes are on us. I feel every set, homing in on the woman by my side.

"Ah," a deep rumble comes from my left. A man in his sixties stops in front of us. His balding head only offers a glimpse of gray, while his protruding belly distends, making the buttons of his shirt look like they're about to pop. "Is this one for sale?"

Lucille stiffens beside me. "No," I bite out, keeping my tone ice cold. If I were to show any emotion, they'd know there's more to this than meets the eye. "She's owned," I tell him. "A good slave, obedient." I ensure the word is a low growl, one Lucy can hear. My little mouse has to play this part perfectly, or she will end up int he clutches of a monster far worse than I am.

"Let us see the obedience you've trained in her," he orders. "You look too young to truly know how to treat one of these." He runs his knuckles down her arm, and I find I'm proud of her for not flinching. Lucille is stronger than she thinks, stronger than I thought she was. I'm surprised, but I'm also fucking hard for her right now.

She doesn't cave in when he tangles his fingers in her hair, and tugs her head back. The old fucking bastard leans in and I'm simmering with rage. It's barely contained, but when I meet the eyes of my contact, he offers me a small shake of his head. I can't do anything, I can't react, so I watch.

"Drop to your knees, whore," the old man grunts, before he releases her. He straightens, his gaze never straying as he regards Lucille. I wait for her to respond, but she doesn't. Instead, she drops to her fucking knees for him, and I want nothing more than to rip the clothes from my body and howl because jealousy is currently burning a hole right through me.

The hiss of his zipper is the last straw before I step in front of Lucille. "The only dick she chokes on is mine," I tell him. "Is that something you'd like to watch? Because you're more than welcome to enjoy the show."

He considers this. I can see his mind running through the options. If he refuses, I can get killed. It wouldn't take much for them to make me bleed all over this thousand pound carpet. But then he laughs. It's a hearty chuckle before he grips my shoulder.

"Show us," he tells me, and I can almost feel Lucille's body tensing as she kneels behind me. I never thought I would ever protect her. I didn't think for one moment I would be jealous if another man, a stranger, were to touch her. But my burning blood is evidence I'm fucked. I have feelings for her. As much as I want to deny it, to hide it, I can't.

I turn to her. Those wide, golden eyes hold mine, pleading with me to stop this. But she knows I can't. There is no stopping what's about to happen. I tangle my fingers in her hair and hold her head steady.

I lean in and whisper, "Don't fuck this up." Before I straighten and unzip my suit pants. I can't deny, the thought of her choking on my dick does make me hard. Each time I've fantasized over the past few months, it's been her face I've imagined. "Show these men how much you love my dick," I tell her, my voice louder now, attracting a crowd.

Without debate, she crawls toward me as I step back each time she moves. They love the cat and mouse game, and my little slut enjoys it too. The fire dancing in her eyes makes me smile.

I stop, allowing her to touch me. The heat of her fingers as they wrap around my cock incites a hiss of pleasure to escape my lips. When she finally swallows me, taking me into her throat, I once again twist my fingers in her hair, and I force my dick even deeper. Her body convulses, along with her throat which only makes my balls twinge with the need to seed her.

I've been with many women, but none have gotten wet like she does from the rough treatment. They like the domineering personality, but when it comes down to it, they can't handle my needs.

With my free hand, I pull my blade from the back of my belt, and I slide it over her pretty cheek as her eyes widen in shock. The men who watch gasp, and I'm certain every one of them are fucking hard.

Lucille pins me with a glare as she chokes. I thrust time and again, and she takes me. She fucking submits and my knees almost give out. Her throat tightens, convulsing around the head of my cock as she gags.

The sound is the only one in the room because every pair of eyes are on her. Even the women, the slaves to be auctioned, are watching. When I feel her nearly puke, I pull my dick from her mouth and shove the wetness into my pants before zipping up.

"I trust this satisfies your morbid curiosity." My stare is on the man who wanted to use her. The bastard laughs out loud before applauding our act in the middle of the room.

"Beautiful. Too bad she's taken." He seems genuinely saddened by this. But I don't give a shit. I help Lucille to her feet, before pulling her against me.

"Good girl," I whisper in her ear before moving toward our contact who's waiting with a grin on his face.

"Nice show," he tells me under his breath. "Let's talk outside."

I follow him, knowing whatever he has to say, will be an answer to all our questions.

Twenty
CROW

H<small>E'S NOT PART OF THE MAFIA, THE</small> B<small>RATVA, BUT HE IS</small> close the Pakhan which makes this easier. I didn't want to come tonight, but since we've been the only ones to meet face to face, it made this easier.

"Quite the show," Aldrick says as he turns to regard both myself and my little mouse. Lucille merely smiles, playing her part perfectly as she looks up at him from under her lashes. There's an innocence to her, a character she's taken on which makes me hard as fuck.

"You can talk normally now," I inform her with a small smile as I regard our contact. The man I've known for far too long. "This is Aldrick. He's been our contact for a number of years, and I trust him with my life."

"You work for the Bratva?" she gasps, shock lacing her tone. Those golden orbs shimmer with interest. I can't stop the jealousy from coursing through me. I know she has no interest in him, at least, I hope she doesn't, I can't deny I want to fucking hide her away for nobody else to see.

"No," he tells her. "I'm working undercover for a client." His explanation is all he can offer because anything more could be detrimental to his life. He's been in the inner circle for years, but they will kill him without second thought. More than I can even count. The man is nearing his fifties, and yet, he's still doing this shit.

"And you know The Fallen?"

He nods with a smile. "I do. I've known them for a long time. They are good men." Even though he means it, I don't feel it. I've never been good, even before the shit went down with my family. As much as I wanted to be the good son, I never was.

"What can you tell me?"

"There are talks of Mahoney having paid for the escape with his daughter's life. There are no final contracts signed, but I have a feeling Volkov doesn't give a shit. He's going to take what he was promised." The words linger in my mind, and I can't imagine what my little mouse is feeling. It's her father. I'm aching to kill him, to watch him bleed out, I know nothing will ever bring me close to finding my brothers.

"My father really is selling me off to the highest bidder" she murmurs, the pain in those few words slices at my chest. It's as if she's taken a knife and wounded me without thought.

"And he's coming here?" I question, trying to focus on the task at hand. We don't have long. If I spend too much time worried about Lucille, I won't get what I came for.

"I'm sending all the intel to Falcon, but I needed you to see the faces of the men who will most likely be at the meeting where Mahoney hands over his daughter." The affection in Aldrick's eyes as he regards the beauty beside me sets me on edge. There is no stopping this. Even if we tried, Mahoney's already made fucking promises. You don't vow to do something for the Bratva, and then break the promise.

"What if I refuse?" Lucille pipes up suddenly, causing us both to glance at her. "What if I'm already married or taken?"

I don't know what she's playing at. There aren't any men who would lay down their lives to save her. But as I think it, I already know who she has in mind—Falcon. He would fucking do it too. My best friend is infatuated with her, and he will do anything to save her life, even go against everything we stood for.

Granted, I've also broken the plan. I've fucked it into hell and now I've had her, I can't let her go. There are so many things wrong with this scenario. I want so much to send her into the darkness and let her go. But I can't.

"No," I say. "She doesn't need to be married. If she's already—"

"There is nothing you can do," Aldrick tells me. I already knew this, but the fear in her eyes made me ask. The panic had gripped me painfully, and it's the only reason I even considered this fucked up plan. There is no way we can marry her, claim her, and send the Bratva packing.

No criminal organization will ever walk away from an agreement. Especially when they've already done the service. Payment needs to be made.

"When is this happening?" I can't be sure about anything, and I know Aldrick will also be in the dark, but I find the tension in my shoulders and the anxiety in my gut needing to ask the question.

"Well, Mahoney still needs to board a flight. I sent Falcon all the tracking details. He'll know the moment Mahoney leaves the bunker. If he so much as steps out into fresh air, we will all know. Volkov may not know what Mahoney's daughter looks like, but he's waiting, very fucking impatiently."

"I can't go with him," Lucille tells Aldrick as if he has the power to stop this. Not even I have so much power because if I did, I would. There is no longer any doubt in my mind I would stop her being taken. Falcon was right, I'm fucked.

"We will fix this," I tell her before looking at Aldrick who only smiles. "Can you send us all the information you have on Volkov?"

"I can. I'll get it done before the night is over. The only thing I want to say is to be careful because these men are no longer playing around. When Mahoney got taken in, they lost their influx of stock," he tells me, using the word stock as if he were talking about shares or possessions. He's talking about the children Lucille's father was stealing.

'Don't worry," I tell him. "This bastard will never see the light of day again. When we find him, he will beg for mercy."

"You don't know what the word means. Do you, Crow?" Aldrick smirks as he regards me. He's known me far too long for me to even try to deny it.

I shake my head slowly, glancing between both Lucille and Aldrick. "No, there will never be mercy for the men who have spent their lives thinking they can hurt without consequence."

There's a small smile on Lucille's face which makes me want to hold her. She grew up with a monster. I blamed her, as well as her father for the pain we'd been through, but she was a victim as much as we were. As much as my parents, my brothers were.

"Be careful," Aldrick tells me before he shakes my hand and leaves both me and Lucille behind. The chill in the air causes her to shiver, and as much as I want to, I can't even offer her my coat because it will be seen as a sign of weakness.

These men will do anything to break a woman. They will bask in the glory of watching blood and tears drip from her body. I may enjoy the control, I may be slightly demented in my needs, but there are limits. I will never admit to them publicly.

"Thank you," Lucille says suddenly, capturing my attention. "For everything."

"I didn't do anything," I tell her, shrugging off the way she looks at me. "I don't deserve thanks for anything." There is no doubt in my mind she cares for me, Falcon, and Hawk. We've not entirely been loving and affectionate toward her.

"You've given me a life to be unashamed about," she tells me as those golden eyes lock on mine. I never expected a woman to ever look at me the way she is right now. But more so, I never *wanted* it before. Never craved the attention of someone like her. She's light. She seems to illuminate the darkest fucking night.

"Don't look at me like that," I tell her adamantly. I keep my tone schooled, icy, like she's used to, but I have a feeling this woman has already seen through it all. I didn't want anyone to know I felt something for her.

But Falcon knew.

Hawk saw it coming a mile away.

Yet, I still fight it, even in this moment.

"Why do you do that?" Lucille questions, her voice soft and gentle as it washes over me as if offering me salvation.

"What?"

"You hide behind a mask," she tells me as if she's reading my fucking mind. "Even though you want me, you push it to the side and act as if I'm nothing more than a distraction to you."

"You are," I tell her earnestly. Even if I did feel anything for her, she's distracting me from work. If I were here with a paid whore, I would have left her to get ravaged by violent men while I did what I needed to—work. Instead, I'm here with Lucille making sure nobody touches her.

"But you still hate me?" The question she throws at me is so innocent, so fucking sweet, I want to choke it out of her. I want to snuff the light from those golden eyes and turn them black as night. I've never wanted to destroy and protect anyone as much as I do her.

"Don't confuse my need for answers, my need to kill your father for my lust for you." I turn to her, hoping she'll listen because I will not say this again.

I'm about to voice my feelings when a hand slaps my shoulder so hard, I almost shift. The heavy touch sets me on edge I don't like people—other than my brothers or Lucille—touching me.

I spin on my heel and find a man I've never seen. He's watching Lucille with more intent than I care to enjoy. He should walk away, but I have a feeling he's not going to. He stops in front of us, his cigarette hanging from his lips as his gaze tracks her from head to toe.

"I want this one," he speaks, but doesn't look at me. His focus is on my girl. I shouldn't feel as if she is mine, but I do. I'm not entirely selfish, but it seems tonight I am. Lucille has come into my life and turned it on its fucking head.

"She's taken," I tell him, not even bothering to look at my girl. Fuck, I need to stop calling her that.

"Aww come on," he moans, chuckling when I grab Lucille's arm and drag her toward the front of the house. We should leave. There's a twisting in my gut telling me this is a bad idea. I've already got what I came for. I should leave. We should leave. Her shoes clack against the cool cobbles as I drag her back to the car. The moment we reach the side of the house, the asshole descends.

He is drunk. I'm not. I spin on my heel, releasing Lucille from my hold before throwing the keys at her. But she doesn't move. Her gaze is locked on the fucker taking a swing at me. I dip low, remembering what Hawk taught me about close up combat.

I swing a left, then a right, making contact with his face easily. Because he's intoxicated, he's not focused. It's easy for me to take advantage of the fact. I am hyper aware of Lucille's gaze burning a hole in my back, but I don't look at her. I know the moment I glance her way, I've given him too much leeway.

So, instead of telling her to leave, I allow her to watch me lose my shit. I kick out, my shoe slamming right into his crotch sending him to his knees. That's when she races forward, her hand on mine as I pull out my blade. She knew I had it on me, she knew I would use it.

With one small glance over my shoulder, I smile before turning to the man before me and I slice through his cheek. The skin parts, in a sinister sliver of flesh. Blood pours from the wound, and Lucille is right beside me. Her dress is getting drenched in crimson as I continue to cut the man up into tiny ribbons.

The deep red of flesh, and the soft hiss of the blade cutting through the skin, hitting bone every now and then is enough to have me blacking out. But her hand lands on my arm, holding me to the present, but allowing me into the darkness where I need it most.

This is where I'm more like myself. When the body finally drops to the ground in a thud, pieces of a man lie at our feet, I turn to her. Those golden eyes shimmer in the low light hides us in the shadows.

Her pupils are dilated. While her mouth is parted, and her flesh is smattered with drops of red. She's never looked more beautiful. That's a lie, the last time she was so exquisitely breathtaking was when we claimed her as ours.

As much as she probably wants to escape The Fallen, I'm almost certain she knows she never can.

.

Twenty One
LUCILLE

Blood drips from my face. Crow looks like a villain, a dangerous, volatile animal who has devoured his prey. It seems I'm next on the menu. He stares at me, the darkness flashes in his eyes makes the silver turn to gunmetal gray.

An icy wind sends shivers through me, my spine tingles with awareness. Crow saunters toward me as his gaze holds me hostage. I can't move. I'm frozen to the spot. He stops inches from me, his hand gripping my hair, tugging me closer as he leans in. His mouth captures mine, the sweetness of his tongue laps against my mouth. His flavor warms me in the cool night as I open for his demanding need.

His body pushes me against the wall, the bricks biting into my back, and his hands trail over my curves until he finds the hemline of my dress as he shoves it up. Once it bunches to my hips, he finds my wetness, the material of my panties drenched from watching him kill.

My demons dance, they sing when his hardness presses against my core. I want so much more.

"Is this what you wanted?" he questions, his voice low and gravely. "Is this what your little cunt needs?" Crow's eyes are filled with lust so dark it sends a cold shiver down my spine.

"Please," I beg, finding myself rolling my hips against his. A hiss of desire escapes his lips and causes me to clench my thighs. My panties are soaked, as his fingers find my pussy, and he shoves the material to the side. With two fingers, he dips both digits inside me.

"That's it, little slut," Crow coos as he finger fucks me deep and fast. His hand moving against my clit, sending spasms of bliss shooting through every inch of my body.

My hands hold onto his shoulders, my nails digging into the bunched up muscle tight with tension. His mouth captures the hot flesh of my neck and his teeth graze along my column. He bites down, sucking the sensitive spot so hard, my eyes roll back in my head as an orgasm takes over me.

Waves crash as I ride out the pleasure. Crow pulls his fingers from my body and brings them to his lips. I watch with hooded lashes as he sucks the arousal from both digits. His lips wet with a mixture of saliva and my juices.

"So fucking delicious," he tells me as the corner of his mouth tilts upward. Sinister lust turns his expression from desire to something far more dangerous. His other hand raises into view, and it's when I see the knife he used on the man who's lying dead on the floor. Blood coats the metal, crimson darkening the weapon. Crow places the wetness onto my cleavage and slides the sharp edge down my dress.

The material is easily sliced, and with every movement, there's a slight nick against my flesh. When he reaches my mound, my heart is thudding wildly against my ribs. I can't describe the need taking a hold of me, but when Crow leans in and licks the blood from my skin, and brings his lips to mine, I devour him. The metallic flavor bursts on my tongue, mingled with his masculine scent.

The blade kisses along my thigh, the chilled metal grazing the sensitive spots turning me molten with need. "Please, Crow," I plead, my desire dripping along my inner thighs.

"Can you two get your shit together?" Falcon's voice cuts through the darkness, cuts through all the need, and when Crow pulls away, we find Hawk and Falcon staring at us.

"What are you doing here?" Crow asks, his tone filled with frustration.

"We need to get the fuck out of here," Falcon informs us. "The fuckers have called in reinforcements. They know she's Mahoney's daughter." Crow doesn't waste time. He grips my arm, tugging me along, ignoring the fact my dress is no flying open. The chill of the night skating along my bare flesh, my nipples hardened from both the cold and the desire which was only moments ago burning me from the inside out.

When we reach the car, he practically shoves me into the passenger seat before slipping into the driver's side after shrugging off his jacket. We follow the other black Maserati which I know to be Falcon's.

"What's going on?"

"There are men coming to find us," Crow says, his grip holding onto the steering wheel. "I killed one of the soldiers."

"But he—"

"They don't give a shit about what he did. This man is one of their trusted soldiers. Anything we've done to them means we have started a war. It means your father knows where you are."

"He's coming," I whisper, the knowledge of the man who destroyed so many lives will soon be here doesn't set me at ease. My gut twists with nervous

214

energy. I'm not sure if I'm showing it on my face, but Crow reaches over, his hand landing on my thigh.

"It's going to be okay," he tells me confidently before he shoves his jacket at me. "Put this on, I can't concentrate on driving with your beautiful tits out and the blood all over your porcelain skin."

I slowly pull on the large coat, which drowns me in warmth. His cologne intoxicates me, calming me. I know I'll never be able to escape him, or my feelings have slowly grown for him. I don't know much about his story, but I do know I was there when my father took his brothers. I'm the reason his family was targeted because my father knew how to get into the house.

"Get out of your head, little mouse," Crow says, using the nickname he's given me. When we're fucking, he calls me his slut, but when we're having a normal conversation, I'm a mouse.

"Why?"

"Because if you continue to panic about this, I'm going to have to distract you," he informs me. I don't know how he'll do that, but something tells me it will have something to do with the knife he likes to play with.

I glance over at him. "What about the guys?"

"They'll be present, because they will be helping me." Desire warms my flesh, tingling my spine, reminding me they all enjoy sharing. I've watched them touch and kiss each other. I enjoyed it. It turned me on.

"I don't even know what to say anymore."

"You've come to the conclusion our hatred has merit," Crow says nonchalantly. He knows how I feel. He knows what I'm thinking. It's as if he can read me like a book, and I'm lying open for him, my pages clear as day. I ponder briefly if the other two can see right through me as well.

"I have," I admit. "But I'm also scared you'll kill me in the end. Even after all this is over and my father is no longer a threat to you." There's no longer a reason to lie to him or to hide how I'm feeling.

"He's never been a threat to me, or to the guys," he informs me. "Our hatred forces us to seek vengeance." He doesn't look at me again, and I'm surprised at how much I miss his attention on me. I crave it. Over the time I'd been around these men, seeing their pain, it's made me more empathetic toward them. To what they've been through. I could never fix what my father did, but the guilt I'd lived with had always forced me to question my own morals. My own darkness.

"I always believed I was evil like him," I admit to Crow. I have never told anyone about this before. Now I'm alone with him, as we drive through the darkness, I find it easier to admit.

"You're not," Crow tells me suddenly, his no-

nonsense tone surprising me. "I thought you were, I believed you had to pay." With a quick glance my way, he doesn't smile, he doesn't offer me any reassurances, but I don't expect it from him because Crow isn't the type of person to gift them. He doesn't give anyone anything he can't or doesn't want to give.

"And now?" I can't stop myself from asking. Deep down, I want him to care about me. I want him to save me and keep me for himself. For all three of them. When I first arrived, all I wanted to do was escape, but watching him tonight, learning more about what they do, I find myself enthralled by them.

"And now I don't know," Crow admits when he pulls into the driveway of the manor house. It's quite exquisite from outside. With the soft golden glow of the lights shimmering in the windows, my breath is stolen when I take in the house I'd been living in.

"I can handle that," I tell him. "But it scares me."

"You're not afraid of me, but you are scared of me not wanting you," Crow says, it's as if he's reading my mind and it's disconcerting. I don't want him to see my emotions. I can't allow him to see how I feel about him, but he's already read me like the back of his hand.

"I don't want to die," I tell him before pushing

open he car door and exiting the vehicle. But I should know better than to run from a hunter. Crow is behind me, his steps hot on my heels as he follows me into the house. Falcon and Hawk are in front of us, and I want to escape with them, but Crow's hand shoots out and grips my bicep.

"Don't you fucking walk away from me, little mouse," he bites out, his tone turning hard. "I'm not done talking to you."

"I am done talking to you," I tell him. "I can't do this, Crow."

His gaze flashes. I know what's he's waiting for, but I cannot give it to him. However, I have a feeling Crow won't let this go easily. He's not a man who can walk away from a challenge. He finally asks, "Do what?"

The man before me needs the words. He wants my admission. Something I cannot give him. Something I know he'll use against me if he knows. He'll hold it over my head while I beg for mercy. But the thing is, Crow doesn't know about mercy. Tonight has made it clear.

"Nothing," I whisper, but his free hand grips my neck, his fingers curl around the column until the tips of his fingers dig into the soft flesh, stealing my breath. My lungs struggle as he pushes me up against the pillar which holds up the balcony sitting above us.

"Tell me what the fuck you're talking about," Crow commands in a tone so drenched in violence, my stomach unfurls in a flurry of nervous energy.

"If I tell you," I answer, "you'll only hurt me."

"But you like it when I hurt you," he throws back easily. There is no longer a debate here. He knows me. He looks directly into my eyes making every part of my body warm. Our earlier tryst is still fresh in my mind and the scent of blood is still burning my nostrils.

"I do," I admit, feeling my cheeks burn with embarrassment. "I have never told anyone about my proclivities."

"Because you're scared."

I nod.

"You don't need to be. Not with us," he informs me before squeezing even harder until my head swims with the lack of air. I'm close to passing out, and my pussy is pulsing for him to fill me. I want him inside me as he makes me lose all focus. "Because we will give you what you need." Crow leans in as my head spins. "You like it rough. You like it dirty, and your little cunt drips when I abuse it. Doesn't it, little slut?"

He releases me suddenly and I cough, pulling in much needed air. I can't answer him, not yet because I can't bring myself to look at him. When I'm lost in pleasure, I can ask for what I need, but when my

219

head is clear of the desire swimming in my mind, the shame of wanting the darkness takes a hold of me.

"Tell me," he orders again.

"I don't want to do this," I tell him, but Crow isn't resting until he's gotten what he wants. He grips my arms and spins me around until my front is pressed against the wall beside the door. The bricks scrape along my skin as he bunches the material of my dress to my hips. My panties are ripped away. "Crow—"

My plea is lost to the night when he kicks my legs apart and his dick nudges my entrance. "If you tell me to stop," he whispers in my ear. "I won't." That's the last thing I hear before his thickness spears me, stretching me painfully. The slick walls of my pussy pulsing around him, wanting to milk him. The need for him to fill me courses through my veins.

He doesn't move slowly, every thrust is brutal, painful. His grip on my hips is going to leave bruises and his fingertips dig into my curves. His mouth is on my neck as he bites down, sucking hard until I feel the skin tear.

A deep growl of bliss vibrates through his chest when I'm pretty sure the flavor of my blood coats his tongue. I'm so close. I'm near the edge, when Falcon steps out onto the patio and smirks at me, watching me get ravaged by his best friend.

"You look fucking exquisite being owned," he tells me with a smirk. He leans forward, and captures Crow's mouth for a quick kiss before his lips find mine, and the metallic flavor bursts on my tongue when he shares the crimson fluid with me.

His fingers trail down my body until he finds my clit, and pinches hard. The pain zaps through me sending me into orbit as I cry out into the kiss. My orgasm erupts without warning, causing my knees to buckle. But I'm caught between the two strong men, who hold me up as I let go.

As my heart beats wildly, I wonder how I'll say goodbye to them once this is over.

Twenty Two
LUCILLE

I KNOW I CAN'T STAY HERE. IF I PUT THEM IN DANGER, I'M only allowing my father to do the same thing he's done so many times before—steal from innocent people. These men kidnapped, brought me to their home, and locked me up, but they had good reason too.

It's so fucked up to even think like that, but it's true.

I pull on a hoodie and make sure I'm covered up. It's cold out and I don't want to freeze before I hit the closest town. I've managed to spy a map in Falcon's office which gave me an idea as to how far I have to go. If I make it there alive, I'll lure my father away from them.

He's after me, so once he has me, he'll forget

all about them. The reminder of what he told them burns my cheeks. The shame of what I had done is every present. I never wanted to be that girl. The memories were so deeply buried, I forced myself to forget them. They've all come crashing back, and I'm filled with the realization I'm a monster, like my father.

I move through the house silently. All the clothes they bought me, everything I leave behind. I don't need it where I'm going. A pang of agony hits me in the chest when I think about walking away from the men who've given me everything I needed. Hawk was slower to accept me, and I understand why.

But even he wanted me here.

They all do.

I would bring them nothing but more agony. I'm a reminder of all they lost. Tears blur my vision and I have to swipe them away. Crying was showing weakness, I can't allow myself to cower from this plan.

When I reach the living room, I find the lock of the patio door easy to open. But before I can step out into the cold, a deep voice resonates from behind me.

"Where are you going?"

A long while ago when I wanted to run to escape them, I thought about how far it would be to the property line. If they'd find me before I even made it

223

halfway. Now though, he's caught me before I even stepped foot out of the house.

I turn to find Hawk staring at me. He's calm, his hands in the pockets of his jeans. The dark material of his T-shirt hugging his muscles as they bunch up. He's broad, toned, and the way his body moves is languid, yet, I know he's dangerous.

His eyes bore into mine. The green almost luminous in the dim light shimmers from the silver moonlight streaming through the windows.

"I can't stay here," I tell him earnestly. "I'm only bringing more heartache on everyone. You've all lost enough without having to deal with my father again."

"You can't leave," he says as if it all makes sense. As if me being here is exactly what I'm meant to be doing. But it's not. He should know it. "If you do go, you'll hurt those two." He gestures with his head to the rest of the house where Crow and Hawk are most probably asleep.

The thought of them alone in bed, warm, safe, it fills me with a sense of satisfaction I never knew before. When I lost the fight with my father for those two boys, Crow's brothers, I felt helpless. But now I can keep him safe, I'm going to do it.

"If you do run, we'll find you before you hit the town. If you make it out here alive. When we do have to chase, we'll only hurt you when we catch you." There is no amusement in his tone. Hawk isn't like Falcon, who jokes around, and he's certainly not like Crow. As serious as they both are, Hawk is stoic.

There is an innate sadness inside him. A pain I don't know anything about. He never told me what happened with my father. I can't force him to either. So instead of asking, I've let it slide.

And it doesn't escape me he doesn't include himself with them when he says they'd be hurt if I left. I don't linger on it for too long though. Hawk does care, to a certain extent. But he prefers the physical to the emotional.

Instead of asking him about his feelings about me leaving, I focus on the real reason for me wanting to walk out. "It's to keep them safe," I say then, my voice cracking on the last word.

Safe. It's an illusion.

Nobody is ever truly safe. We're all walking around with danger lurking in every corner of our lives.

"You shouldn't go," he responds before moving closer to where I'm standing. When he reaches me, he stops, inches from me. His toes hit my black boots. They bought me a pair when we did some online shopping. It was the only time I ever saw anyone else, when the delivery driver pulled up.

Crow was convinced I would scream for help, but instead, I watched my new wardrobe get delivered, and waved the stranger off without so much as a mumble. I don't *want* to leave them. But I need to.

Hawk reaches up, causing me to flinch. I never know what to expect from him, but this time, it's a gentle whisper of his knuckles as they tease their way over my skin. The softness of his affection is apparent in this moment. It steals every breath from my lungs.

"Don't go," Hawk pleads. He actually fucking begs.

"Give me a reason to stay," I whisper, tipping my head back so I'm staring into the endless orbit of those piercing blue eyes.

The air is so thick, I struggle to pull it in. The tender touch of his fingers as they trace a line from my ear to my jaw before he grips my chin between his thumb and forefinger sends heat sizzling through my veins.

"Why?"

"Because I need to know you care too," I breathe the words, and Hawk leans in further. His lips brush along mine. It's not a kiss, it's a whisper, and I pray with everything I have he does steal my mouth, and he devours every inch of me.

"What if I don't care?" he asks me, his tone low, barely audible, but the words are clear, and they break my heart. My chest tightens with pain

226

so acute, my eyes sting with agony. I haven't ever allowed myself to feel, to fall, to want someone. Now, there are three men I would do anything for, and it scares the shit out of me.

"Then I'll go."

"What about them?"

"I care about all three of you," I admit because I can't hide anymore. This isn't something I can fight. Not anymore. If I need to let them go, I will. That's what you do when you love someone. *Isn't it?*

"Why?" Hawk tips his head to the side to regard me for a short moment before he continues, "Because you get good dick? Or because of something else? Like guilt." The words sting like they're meant to. He's trying to hurt me. The other two men have allowed me to tell my story, they listened and understood what happened to me. I've heard their pain, but Hawk wasn't there, he never allowed himself to confess his hate for me may be unfounded.

"Because I'm human, and you're all hurt. I feel empathy because I can't imagine what you went through. If I could change it—"

"No, you don't know what I went through." His hand drops to his side. Those eyes though, the blue shimmers with anger. He could hurt me right now. He could kill me, and yet, I'm not walking away. He needs to see I'm not the monster my father is.

"Tell me," I request in a tone which belies how afraid I am of him. Faking confidence is something I've had to learn to do. It's come in handy now, and as I look up at Hawk, I know as much as he's fighting his feelings, he can't do so for much longer. The expression on his face tells me so, his brows pinched together, his mouth tense as the corner tip downward.

"You're not ready—"

"Fuck not ready," I bite out as anger overtakes me. I'm done being kept in the dark about what he's experienced. "You can't hide forever, Hawk."

His hand slams into my chest as if he's trying to push me away, but my back hits the door, the cool glass rattling behind me. It doesn't hurt, but my breath is knocked from me momentarily.

"You see what I can do," he threatens with a smirk. "I know you like being roughed up," he tells me. "I'll gladly do it, but there will be no pleasure for you."

"Tell me the fucking truth," I hiss, clenching my teeth painfully as my jaw ticks. I don't move his hand; I don't fight him. It's what he wants me to do, but this time, I'm not giving in so easily. I stand tall.

We're at a standoff, and I'm going to win.

Hawk thinks he knows me because I'm what he built up in his mind. It's like children who think there's a monster in the closet, or under the bed. They're convinced it's scary, it's huge, and it's coming for them.

But in all honesty, the monsters aren't under the bed or in the closet.

They're the faces you see every single day.

Those scary things you believe are hidden, are right before you. They walk in the light, in the sunshine. They show you love and affection in one moment and hate in the next. That's what the real monsters are. Hawk knows it, and I know it too.

"It was so long ago," he finally says as he lowers his hand, and I can breathe again. "I shoved it to the back of my mind."

"I know the feeling."

"It's too difficult to fathom," he mumbles. "You think if you lock it in a box and never think of it again you're safe. It's as if it's out of sight and out of mind, all will be well. But it's all a lie."

I nod, but I don't respond anymore. I'm too afraid if I do say something, he'll stop talking. I need him to tell me the story so instead I remain silent. But my gaze never leaves him.

Hawk moves to the sofa and settles in. For a long moment, I don't follow, but when he leans back, I know we're in for the night. So, I lock the door and make my way to the sofa where he's seated.

"I didn't think I would ever hurt so much," he tells me. "Even the time I spent in the Army wasn't near the pain I'd experienced in my past. I left the service because it wasn't helping my anger, it was only making it worse."

"So you came back for Crow and Falcon?"

He nods. "They needed me more than I needed to be out there killing people. But I did find fighting helps ease the rage consuming me at times." He's never spoken like this to me before. Most times, I receive a grunt or a mumble of something but now he's telling me what I need to hear.

"But it returns," I say knowingly. "That need to expel whatever is eating you inside, it comes back time and again."

Hawk's gaze meets mine, and he finds a kindred spirit. It's the same thing I feel when I need the rough, the manhandling. It's strange how I focus the energy on sex, but it's how I cope. It's how I've always coped.

"Sometimes, it scares me how much I want it though. I'm afraid one day, I'll do it to someone innocent."

"You're not a monster, Hawk," I insist gently. "You're a good person who went through something traumatic."

His gaze snaps to mine. "Every single time I'm in the ring, I picture your father in there with me. I see his face in every man I beat up. I enjoy it. The blood lust, the violence courses through me. It makes me livid, but it also satiates my craving."

I don't want to venture into his darkness. I don't want to make him say anything he doesn't want to. Instead of demanding he tell me everything, I whisper, "Will you tell me what happened now?"

Twenty Three
HAWK

"**W**ILL YOU TELL ME WHAT HAPPENED NOW?" Her whispered plea makes me cave. Being close to her, knowing she wanted to leave sets me on edge. I don't want her to go, to leave us, but I also struggle being around her.

"I've never told anyone outside of The Fallen about this," I admit. It's true, my brothers are the only ones who have ever heard my story. Even then, they've never brought it up again. They may have experienced pain, but they both know mine has cut my soul in half. It's as if a part of me is missing, and I'll never get it back.

I'm not sure I want it back.

What do you do with something so tainted, so blackened, nothing can cleanse it of the darkness? I've believed it my whole life. I'm certain it's the reason I hate her so much. She's light. Her fucking name means light. But even she can't heal me. She can't fix what her father broke inside me.

"If you don't feel—"

"The night he came into our house, after he sent you away, you waited in the car," I tell her. I can see her nodding silently beside me, so I continue. "He saw me, hit me over the head with the butt of the gun. When I was weakened, he bound me to my sister's desk chair. The fucking thing was tiny, but he managed to get me secure."

The more I speak, the deeper I dive into the horror of that night, the more my chest tightens. It's as if a weight is lying on me, holding me down like he did.

"I screamed for him to stop, but he only laughed." My voice cracks when I recall every single second.

Tears roll down my cheeks as I watch him slice her nightdress. The soft white cotton falling away and her delicate body shaking as he takes in the prize. The sick fucker is going to die. I'm going to make sure of it.

I fight against the bindings holding me in place, but I can't get free. The thick rope cuts into my arms. I'm pretty sure I'm bleeding, but I don't care. I need to save her. I need her to be okay.

233

"You see," he tells me with satisfaction in his tone. "The idea was to come in and get out," he says. "But since you decided to fuck up my plans. I'll make you watch." He laughs out loud, the sound vibrating through me, as if he's struck me.

"No! Leave her the fuck alone!"

He ignores my screams. As he gently moves to each corner of her bed. She's staring at me. Her eyes wide, her mouth parted in sobs of fear. I want to tell her it's going to be okay, but it's not. Nothing will ever be okay again.

My folks won't be home for hours. The girl he sent out isn't going to call for help. She was here helping him. I don't know who she is, but they'll both pay. I don't care if I have to hurt her too. He leaves Missy and turns toward me. I'd rather have the pain than watch her in agony.

He takes a few steps toward me and stops in front of me. I can see the bulge in his pants which makes my stomach lurch and I recoil from his touch.

"Both boys and girls need to learn how to do things," he tells me. "Do you want to learn?"

"Fuck you!" My voice is stronger now. If I can keep his attention on me, I can hopefully save Missy. His hand lands on my cheek so swiftly, I didn't see it coming. The sting of pain slices through every inch of me. The moment I get loose I'm going to make him bleed. I'm going to carve out his fucking intestines.

"Now," he whispers when he leans in, his mouth close to my ear. "Did you want to watch while I show

your sister how good it is to be a woman?"

Bile rises up from my gut, and I choke on the acid as it burns my throat. The putrid flavor spilling from my lips when his big, rough hand lands on my crotch. He attempts to rub me, but my revulsion doesn't allow my body to betray me.

His free hand grips the back of my head and he forces my face against his zipper. A hiss falls from his lips as tears burn my eyes. I refuse to cry, but everything inside me is filled with pure rage. When I'm angry, I cry.

He continues rubbing me, trying to get me hard. "Don't you like her smooth, pretty little cunt?" he whispers. "I bet it's so damn tight. It will feel like a glove sucking you in. Have you thought about it? Mm?"

His ministrations continue. His hand grips me, stroking, getting me to half mast, and I fight it with everything I have. Whatever the fuck is happening to me is wrong. I hate it. I'm broken. Why is this happening to me? Guilt and shame blur together in a whirlwind of agonizing lies. I am not this person. I'm nothing like this monster who's stolen our home.

"You see, little girl," the bastard murmurs. "Your brother likes the sight of your pretty body. So smooth, so tight," he says with a chuckle which has my stomach rolling, fighting the revulsion, I bite down on his leg earning me an ear splitting slap sends me to the ground.

I expect him to beat me up, to hurt me, but he turns on his heel and makes his way to the bed where my sister *is screaming for me to help her. I'm helpless to watch. The horror which continues before me is more than painful, it's more than any fucking agony you could put me through.*

The bastard stands once more, his body drenched in her blood, the knife in his hand soaked in the crimson fluid of my sister's life, he smiles down at me. In my mind, I vow to myself I will seek vengeance. I'll make him watch as I hurt the girl he had with him. I know it's his daughter, there was a closeness to them. But I'll wait until she's of age, until she thinks she's safe, I'm going to make her fucking pay while this monster watches.

"I spent my life waiting and watching you," I tell her. When I look up to see why Lucille's so quiet, I notice her shock, her revulsion, and her empathy. There is no pity in her eyes, and it calms me. I don't like pity.

"I…" Her voice trails off, silence hangs between us like a weight. It's heavy, commanding every breath I take. "I can't… I don't…" She shakes her head, her body trembling as her hands fumble at the hoodie she's wearing. Her fingers tangle in the soft fabric, and I know she's still processing.

When I first told the guys, they were livid, but it took them some time to come to terms with what I told them. "I wanted to hurt you so much," I admit to her. "The hate I felt for you, it overshadowed everything. All those times I watched you from the shadows, when you bumped into me after leaving the bar, I wanted so much to shove you against a wall and slice you open."

I don't hold back and neither does she. "I don't blame you for wanting to do it." I'm surprised by her admission.

"Falcon and Crow saw you as something different than how I looked at you. They saw a woman. I saw the monster. I couldn't differentiate between you and him. I wanted you to suffer like Missy did."

Lucille moves from the one sofa, and settles in beside me. Her hand on my leg makes me anxious, but I don't push her away. I want to, but I also want to drag her closer. To feel her body against mine. I want to lose myself in her and forget.

But forgetting means I'm not fulfilling my vow. I look up to see her watching me. It looks like she's expecting me to hurt her, waiting for it. I grip her wrist, twisting it until she's whimpering, and I drag her over to straddle me. Her legs on either side of mine.

"If you need this," she whispers, leaning in, she tips her head to the side, and I note Crow's teeth marks on her neck. "I accept it." Three words are like gasoline to my anger. She drenches me in her fuel, and I grip her hips, digging my fingers in until she makes more pained sounds which make my dick hard.

The corner of my mouth tips upward, as I watch her squirm. The tears forming in her eyes are pretty gemstones, glistening with agony. I tug her forward, then back. Her heat against my crotch. I'm hard, so fucking hard.

"This is what you want. Isn't it?" I hiss as she moans. There's no denying this woman loves the rough shit. She hungers for it. Like a craving which can never be satiated. "You're never leaving us." There's no lie in my words. The truth is, I don't want her to leave, but I don't tell her, not yet.

Releasing her hip, I tangle my fingers in her hair and tug her head back until the smooth column of her neck is bared to me. The scent of her is intoxicating. Like the first shot of whiskey burning all the way down.

With my other hand, I dart it between her spread thighs, and I rub against the crotch of her sweatpants. The warmth emanating from her makes me smile. Her whimpers and moans get louder the harder I stroke against her clit, and as she crests, I stop.

Her lashes flutter, and her mouth parts on a pained mewl, and I start again. The edging is going to have her in pain very fucking soon. She's hungry for an orgasm. Each time I deny her, the sounds she makes has my cock throbbing against my zipper.

My fingers dip into her, pushing the material inside her body, soaking it in her arousal. Wetness and warmth. This woman is pure evil, making me want, making me hunger for a taste. Each time we've all fucked, I haven't touched her, but right now, as her cunt drenches through her underwear and the joggers she's wearing, I want so much more.

She rolls her hips, trying to get friction where she needs it. But once again, I deny her by pulling my hand away. She can't look at me because I have her head tipped back, and I can't stop myself from leaning in and sucking the soft flesh of her neck into my mouth. I don't go near Crow's marks on her, I create my own. My teeth graze along the delicate column, biting and sucking until she's crying out.

Her thighs tremble against mine. Her hands hold onto my shoulders as if I'd let her go now. The admission I offered her was so she can understand my anger. I didn't think I'd ever confess what happened to anyone else. But with Lucille, I knew I had to.

My brothers have chosen her, claimed her. She's not going anywhere, and I know I need to accept it. Crow may have wanted her dead, but the plan is long gone.

I don't blame him though. We've never met a woman who can keep up with us. We haven't ever had a woman who asked for more. Most of them would run a mile when they learned what we desire, but Lucille begs for it.

"Please, Hawk," she begs, her body convulsing over mine. She's teetering on the edge of insanity. Her body must be aching, the pain so acute, I'm pretty sure if I were to slip my hand in her panties, she'd explode.

"What?"

"Please, I need it." Lucille is a dirty girl, asking to come like a common slut. Her hips undulate, her hands grip my shirt, trying to pull me closer, but I don't move. She's not strong enough to overpower me. There is no way she can top from the bottom, not with me.

"Need what? Tell me," I coax as my fingers trail over her nipples, and I pinch one, twisting until she's screaming out my name. Her words incoherent when she speaks as I taunt the other hardened bud.

I release her hair and she's finally able to look at me. Her eyes are shimmering, pupils dilated as she regards me. "Please fuck me," she says then, her tone confident.

Her hands are already fighting my zipper before I have time to respond. Her hand wraps around my cock, causing a hiss to escape my lips. I don't think twice about ripping her sweatpants creating a gap where I shove her panties to the side, and she sinks down on my dick.

The warmth, the tightness, her fucking juices coating my cock sends my mind into orbit. Euphoria warms my blood, heating every inch of me as she takes me to the hilt. For a second, she doesn't move, and then, her hips roll.

Lucille bounces on my dick, and I watch in awe as this blonde, golden eyed beauty takes from me and gives me pleasure in return. Nothing but pure desire races through my veins. I grasp her hips, moving her back and forth.

"Fuck," I bite out as her walls pulse. She's close, I am too. It doesn't take long for me to thrust my hips, fucking her deeper, harder, faster. The sounds of us fucking echoes through the room, and suddenly, her body starts shaking, and her cunt squeezes my dick, milking the ever living fuck out of me.

I empty my seed, as she soaks my cock.

Hot, fast breaths come from both of us, and I know I've taken the final plunge into the depths. There is no going back. This girl is ours. She's never leaving our side.

Twenty Four
FALCON

WHEN MY PHONE BUZZES ON MY DESK, I GLANCE DOWN to find Dante's name flashing on screen. He only calls when he has intel for me, so I pick it up, hoping there are answers for us.

"What have you got for me?"

He chuckles on the other end of the line and the deep rumble has me pondering more about his sexual nature than the work we're talking about. He reminds me so much of Crow. All our interactions have had me more intrigued each time.

"We found the Pakhan," he says. "He's heading your way soon. Mahoney has left the bunker in Los Angeles, and he's making his way to the airstrip. I would say within the next twenty-four hours, you'll have him to deal with."

"So he is coming for her."

"He is," he affirms, and I imagine him nodding. "I spoke to Drake, and he's willing to step in if you need us. I have a team at the ready, say the word and we'll be there to take the fucker down. We'll fly out tonight."

I ponder this for a long moment. I know Crow trusts Dante, so it won't be an issue if I take the lead on this and agree. Knowing we're up against a fucking criminal organization like the Russian mafia, we will need all the help we can get.

"That sounds good," I tell him. "We have men who can step up, but this is personal, and if we can double up our force, I'm hoping we can put an end to all of them easily, and quickly."

"Our past is littered with men like this, men who think they can exert their power over young children, over anyone they deem weaker, so we will definitely be there. You don't have to doubt us," he assures me, and I settle back as my office door opens and Crow stalks in.

I hang up once we're confirmed and open up a new email to get the address to Dante. Both Savage brothers will be here to help, along with their teams. It will give us the upper hand when it comes to dealing with Mahoney and his boss.

"Who was that?" Crow settles into the armchair across from my desk. His stare tethered with mine.

"Dante says he and his brother can be here tomorrow with back up. I agreed," I tell him. "If we're taking on the mafia, we may as well have reinforcements should we need it."

Crow nods slowly, his focus turning to the window before flicking back to mine. "What about this job we were hired for? We haven't heard back from him yet?"

"I have a feeling it was a distraction. I looked into him, Simmonds is a banker, straight-laced, nothing on him which didn't make sense until I saw where he worked."

"Where?" Crow leans forward, elbows on his thighs, those metallic orbs, holding mine hostage.

"Bank of Switzerland, offshore accounts," I explain. When I saw this on his profile, I knew there was more to the man than needing a hitman for his wife cheating, or something similar. This is someone connected to the job, to Mahoney. I'm sure of it.

"Get him on the phone," Crow says. "Let's either bring him in for questioning, or we get the answers from him on a call. But make sure it's recorded, I want evidence."

"I think bringing him in might be the best idea."

"Why? You want to play torturer again?" Crow's dark brow arches as he watches me, the corner of his mouth tipping into a smirk.

"You know it," I tell him, leaning back in my

chair. He keeps his focus on me, "What's wrong with you?"

"We need to tell her," he admits slowly. He is right. I know he is, but I honestly don't want to talk about the past. As much as I know I should, especially to Lucille, I can't bring myself to confess the memories still hold me hostage.

"Now?"

Crow is silent for a moment. "Maybe. If she's going to stay here, be a part of our family, she needs to know the truth. If she decides she wants to leave—"

"She won't."

"How can you be so sure?" he challenges as he regards me. An arched brow lifting in question. "Because what we've all been through isn't easy to listen to, and it's not easy to accept."

"She's not like that, she won't run when things get tough."

The corner of his mouth quirks. "You have a lot of confidence in her," he tells me.

"And you don't?" I throw back, but he only grins. He can't deny it. She's stronger than we all expected. She's innocent. The actions of her father don't mimic who she is. Crow cannot debate that.

"She is ours now," I tell him.

"She is," he agrees with a nod.

I look up at him before saying, "She can't leave

us." The fear Lucille will walk away is present in my mind. I've thought about it far too much. We were determined to make her pay, to ensure her father pays, but she's not guilty of wrongdoing. You can't change who your family is, and you certainly can't change who your parents are.

Crow pulls out his phone as he flops onto the sofa. I watch him with a smile as he takes a selfie, then hits send on what I can only imagine is a message to Lucille. We gave her a phone to use while in the house, but it's locked, and we control who she contacts.

His dark hair flops into his eyes making him look like a goddamned Adonis. I've always thought he was good looking, but when Crow is doing something for attention, he's breathtakingly handsome.

It doesn't take long for Lucille to appear at the door to my office. She's dressed in a pair of shorts which show off her long, lean legs. Her body encased in an oversized hoodie hides the rest of her curvaceous figure, but I know what lies under the material.

"What was that?" she questions Crow. This girl has balls of steel, and it makes me laugh. "Selfies to taunt me to obey your commands?"

"Sit," Crow responds, his cold exterior taking over once more. "We need to talk."

I round the desk and settle in beside him. "We needed you to know the story behind our hatred of your father. You know Crow's," I tell her, watching her reaction. A slow, guilt-ridden nod. She was there the night it all went down. "Mine is a little different. We came home right after the first kidnapping which was my sister," I continue as I go back in my memories to the day haunting me. "My mother was out, my father was at work, and I told my sister she shouldn't go out into the garden while the security team were working on checks."

"Falcon and I were out watching Hawk in a fight. The three of us had been inseparable since we got home." Crow leans back, crossing an ankle over the opposite knee.

"It was only when I got to her bedroom and found blood and ripped clothes, did I realize she wasn't there. The signs of a struggle were clear."

"M-my father—"

"He was let in by our security team under the guise of being an installer. They checked his credentials," I tell her. The guilt I lived with since then has slowly blackened my soul. I promised myself I would never let anyone hurt an innocent again.

"That's when we became The Fallen," Crow explains. "The idea of seeing families hurt like ours was not something we could live with."

"Dark angels," Lucille whispers as the name becomes clearer. "And you were out for vengeance."

I nod. "We watched the trial from afar," I explain. "If we had walked into the courtroom, we would've probably been arrested ourselves."

"But patience was what was needed," Crow says. "It may not be our virtue, but we knew if we waited, more would come to light."

"Is that how you knew I would be here? Did you follow me to England?"

"For the most part," I tell her before Crow can jump in. "We all wanted you dead." My words cause her to wince, but I continue on, "We believed you needed to pay for his sins. His actions are and will always be inconceivable. It doesn't matter who he's working for, everyone has choices."

"My father made his choice," Lucille tells us adamantly. "He chose to do the wrong thing, even in court when he could have come forward and apologized, he chose to stay silent. When I looked at him, there was nothing more than satisfaction in his smile. He fucking smiled," she insists, tears brimming her lashes making those golden orbs shimmer.

"I don't know what happened to my sister," I finally admit. "If she's alive, I don't even know if she'll remember a life without the abuse she is most definitely suffering right now. The men who

248

purchase these girls aren't kind. They're monsters."

"I wish I could tell you more," Lucille whispers. "I wish I could give you the closure you need, but he hid so much from me. Even while I stood in Hawk's home, not knowing it was his, I couldn't do anything. The moment he stabbed me, I knew I would be nothing more than a victim to him."

She blinks and sadness trickles down her cheeks. I want to go to her, but I can't bring myself to move. I've never been good at showing emotion, especially when women are crying. Tears of pleasure are very fucking different to the pain I see in Lucille's eyes right now.

"I want to see him bleed," I tell her, hoping it would distract from the heartbreak she's currently experiencing. When she blinks at me and nods, I can't stop myself from dropping to my knees at her side. I hold her face in my hands, keeping her steady so she can't look away. "But you're ours now," I say with confidence. "There is no way you can escape us, even if you tried, we would find you."

"B-but, I just—"

Crow joins me. "There is no debate."

"Isn't there?" Hawk says as he enters the room. He may be angry at our choice, but he will come to terms with it. I know he will. He takes time to get on the bandwagon, but he can also no longer deny she's claimed. We may have stolen her, taken her exactly like her father kidnapped our siblings, but we love her.

The thought causes my breath to halt. The shock on my face must be evident because both Crow and Hawk ask, "What's wrong?" I can't tell them anything yet. We've only now managed to overcome the need to kill her. Even after fucking her, we needed to admit to ourselves she belongs here.

"Nothing," I say before pushing to my feet. "We need to leave."

As I make my move to the desk, my phone buzzes against the wood. The number is hidden on screen, and I wish I were paying more attention because if I was, I could have seen this incoming on the software which will reveal the caller.

"What?" I answer, and deep down, I know who it is before his voice comes across the line.

The dark, demented tone of Mahoney responds, "I want my daughter back."

"What makes you think we're willing to barter?" I ask as I turn to look at the three sets of eyes locked on me. Questions dance in their gazes. "She's ours now."

"Like fuck she is," he spits. "She is the payment I need to ensure my freedom." We already knew this. The man will only be killed if he doesn't deliver what was promised to the Pakhan, and he knows it.

"Your freedom means nothing to us," I inform

him.

Lucille's gaze burns through mine. Her mouth parts as she watches me, and I wonder what's going through her head right now. The fear of seeing her father must be eating her alive.

We, as The Fallen, all we feel is anger. I don't doubt my brothers will be ready to take this bastard on. "Bring her to the warehouse on St. Hovis farm," he tells me. "Or I will have my colleagues pay a visit to your homes in L.A. I still have all the addresses." The threat is clear.

I hang up before he can say anything more. I can't listen to the bastard without my blood boiling over. "He wants Lucille."

The silence greeting me is deafening. Crow's brows furrow, Hawk is his usual stoic self, but I can tell from the way his hands fist at his sides he's not happy. We should wait for the Savage brothers to arrive with back up, but the three of us have faced far worse adversaries before. Mahoney may have the Bratva on his side, but right now, I can't bring myself to give Lucille over to him.

"I'll go."

"Like fuck you will," Crow bites out, his glare snapping to Lucy. I've seen him angry before, but never seen him defend her in this way. We've spoken about killing her before, and he's been all for it.

"I can't let you go," she tells him before pushing

to her feet. "If he wants me, he can take me. I'm not letting anyone else get hurt because of my father, or me." They're at a standoff, both wanting to step up, both needing to control. I didn't expect her to say anything. I thought she would have wanted to run.

But she's surprised me.

"Then we all go," I announce.

"I'm ready to spill some blood," Hawk responds as he cracks his knuckles. The man like to get bloody. I can't wait to see how this showdown is going to go.

"The Fallen have accepted you," Crow informs Lucille, "Now it's time to show you what a real family does."

As he offers her his hand, I know it's done. There is no going back. We have our girl, we have a new addition to our family, and there's no changing it.

Twenty Five
LUCILLE

THE DRIVE OUT OF THE FALLEN PROPERTY IS SILENT. There is a deafening quiet hanging like a weight. It's a reminder we may be walking into a trap. That we may not come back from this alive. As much as I wanted to fight them, I knew they wouldn't let me go.

Sitting in the back with Hawk beside me, while Crow drives and Falcon is settled in the passenger seat makes it feel as if I'm not alone. I spent years convinced I will always be haunted by my father, and now, these men want to take it away. They want to save me even though it was my dad who broke their families apart.

When we pull into the driveway of the farm a few hours later, I'm exhausted. It's late. It's been a long day. There have been confessions and admissions, but the next few hours are going to be even worse.

My gut churns as we exit the vehicle. I'm surrounded by The Fallen. They move in sync as if we're all one person. A door opens and I notice a few cars parked inside, along with one behind the enormous building. But as we take a step closer, gunshots ring out, sending us to the ground. The cold dirt against my face smells of shit, and my stomach rolls at the stench.

I'm dragged by two strong men, while Crow, Hawk, and Falcon are held at gunpoint. The bastards came out of the shadows. They were waiting for us. I knew it was a trap. There's nothing we can do about it now.

Inside, I'm shoved to the floor. The cold concrete bites into my knees, and when I look up, I see my father, beside a man who looks like he could kill me if he merely snapped his fingers.

"Here she is, Volkov," Dad says with a smile. The same sinister glare on his face is the one I used to go to sleep seeing. A nightmare. A deranged man who wants to hurt innocent people.

The man, Volkov, shrugs, taking me in as if I were a piece of furniture he was considering purchasing. "I suppose I can take her."

"No," I shout, but a kick to my ribs has me

reeling. Agony shoots through my side, and I struggle to pull in air, but nobody helps me.

Seeing my father again has bile rising to my throat. I never wanted to look into those dark, evil eyes again. But I can't avoid it. The way his mouth curves upward tells me he no longer cares about what happens to me. I don't doubt the years in prison has changed him even more. The darkness I recognized in my father when I was merely a teenager is still there, it's only more vicious now.

He meets my gaze, his glare locked on me. "It's time you paid for my release, sweetheart," he tells me with confidence dripping from every word. I don't expect anyone to understand the pain of how my father hurt me, but the men who stand behind me, with guns to their heads do. They've accepted me.

"I won't be paying for anything," I answer softly, keeping my voice calm. I hope he doesn't see the fear dancing in my eyes, because I don't doubt there is. "You needed to stay behind bars. You can't be free after what you did."

"Enough!" One of the men in a black suit shouts. His voice is deep, it rumbles like a truck rushing down the highway. It sets me on edge. "Take them," he orders, and the men holding guns on The Fallen step forward. "We are leaving, I can't stand here and listen to this bullshit."

In the next second, all hell breaks loose when shots are fired, and I'm shoved to the ground. I'm not sure what the hell is going on, but the twisting in my gut tells me it's not good.

The scent of metal fills my nostrils when the man my father offered me to grips my arm and drags me toward him. My knees scrape along the cold concrete, and the biting agony slices my flesh has me whimpering.

"Don't you dare fucking touch her." Crow's voice is filled with anger as he shouts into the darkness. "I will fucking kill you." I didn't expect him to fight for me, not like this. He's always been aloof about his feelings. Fucking me isn't loving me. But Crow's tone is tinged in more than vengeance, there is affection in it.

The man holding me, Volkov, glances over his shoulder, the smile on his face is sinister. He regards Crow who's on the floor, a man in a suit holding him down, and says, "She's mine." I'm dragged farther away from the men who've stolen my heart.

I can't fight because I'm trying to stay on my feet. But each time he tugs at me, I stumble forward which only hurts more. Cold ground bites into my sensitive skin. The hold he has on me is going to leave a bruise. At times, Crow marked me, and I wanted it, I loved it. But this is the devil taking me down to hell with him, and I know I won't be able to fight him off. Even if I do, he'll gladly make me regret it.

"Please, let me go," I plead with him when we reach the back of the building and head outside to a waiting SUV with blacked out windows. A sense of dread takes over because I know the moment I'm in the car, I won't ever be able to escape. "My father should never have offered my life. I don't want this, please," but no matter how much I beg, this bastard won't listen to me. So, I tug my arm, which has him stumbling backward, and I managed to dig my heels into the ground before he can get a proper grip on me again.

He spins on his heel, and it's only a second later the harsh sting of his hand makes contact with my cheek. The heavy gold ring on his finger cuts into my lip, and the whoosh of blood fills my mouth, causing me to cough and splutter at the flavor.

"If you don't shut up," he bites out, his teeth grit in rage. "I will make sure you shut up permanently. I don't need your mouth for what I have in store for you." I'm shoved into the car, the soft leather smooth against my face, as blood drips from my mouth and tears stream down my cheeks.

I don't know where I'm going to end up, but the boys won't be able to find me once we leave the country. I have no doubt I'm fucked. As much as I wanted to escape The Fallen, now all I want is for them to find me, to save me and to keep me.

The car doors slam, and I push to sit up on the seat. My focus is still blurry when I blink, trying to clear it to take in the driver. I don't know why, but if I can perhaps get him to look at me, maybe I can plead with him to help me. To save me.

But when I do settle back, my head spins as I take in my predicament. Volkov settles in beside me before I have time to even take note of the driver. The fragrance of my captor's cologne is cloying as it sinks into my senses, overwhelming me. It's a sickly sweet scent which doesn't seem to fit with the man in question. He strikes me as someone who would want to exude power, because it's what he's used to, but the floral notes are all I smell.

He doesn't touch me again, so when I finally glance to my side, I realize he's not even looking at me. I'm nothing more than a possession. Crow warned me these men don't have relationships, the auctions they attend offer them slaves who will obey without debate because they know if they were to answer back, they'd end up with blood and bruises.

As the car pulls away, I want nothing more than to fight, but my trembling hands won't do much damage to the man beside me. With a hold of the material of my tights, I attempt to calm my trembling fingers, but it's no use. I'm far too fucking scared to do anything. I can't sit around and wait for

The Fallen to save me, but I don't know if I have the strength, or the energy to fight Volkov off myself.

I should have taken the blade Crow offered me, but I believed they would save me. There has to be a way to get free because I cannot go with this man. Being owned by a monster will be the end of me.

It's almost comical to think there are three men out there who I considered monsters, and now all I want to do is run back to them. They gave me something nobody else ever has, they showed me who I truly am. I will get free. I have to see them again. One way or another, I will save myself.

As the car weaves through the dark streets, I try to see out the window if there are any lights following behind, but it's blackness which greets me.

"Where are we going?" I chance a question, awaiting the attack once more, but none comes. Volkov glances at me, his eyes dance with darkness. Violence is the only thing this man knows, it's clear. He's not afraid to bestow it on anyone who comes close to him—man or woman, he will make me bleed. I have a feeling he'll enjoy it even more because I *am* a woman.

"You're mine now," he tells me earnestly. The confidence in his tone tells me he always gets what he wants. But it would be understandable because I doubt anyone would want to mess with the Pakhan.

"I'm sure there are many others who would go with you willingly," I tell him, hoping he'll see reason. But I doubt it. A man like him doesn't *need* to listen to anyone below him, because he believes being the ruler, what he does is right. Even when it's wrong.

"Let me make something clear," he tells me. The car takes a left, and suddenly, there are blinding lights speeding toward us. Within seconds, we're rolling over, and over, again. Pain shoots through every inch of me as the crashing of glass deafens me as it echoes through the small space as metal is crushed and bent.

Blood and gas are the only scents infiltrating my senses. It's so strong, my stomach lurches when I try to breathe. Darkness flickers in my vision, but the heat of flames licks close to me. Movement at my side catches my attention, but I can't move. I'm wedged between metal, which holds me down and though I can't feel Volkov beside me anymore, I know he's close. He has to be.

I'm not sure what's going on, but as my vision blurs, panic sets in and my pulse spikes. My lungs struggle to pull in much needed air, and each time I manage a small inhale, everything hurts. I must have a broken rib, or something because it's far too painful to be a fracture.

But I don't know much about broken bones.

I've never been injured like this. Suddenly, there are hands on me, grabbing at me, and when they pull, I cry out as agony shoots through my leg, the warmth of fluid coating my skin tells me something has cut into me. Whether it's metal, or glass, it's sliced me open.

"No!" I cry out once more and the hands disappear.

Then I hear Hawk's voice. "I'll get you out, hold on for me." The panic in his tone sets me on edge. The scent of gas becomes overwhelming. I realize why Hawk is panicking, it could catch fire. Shit.

I'm going to die.

No.

Yes.

I don't know.

My head spins with scenarios as I lay silently, trying to stay calm, but the longer I wait, the more my pulse seems to race, my heart thudding against my ribs painfully. I've never thought about how I would die, but this wasn't it.

A squeal of metal deafens me. Then I hear my saviors. It's not only Hawk, Falcon, and Crow, there are more male voices shouting and screaming as the sound of them trying to break through the broken vehicle to free me takes over.

It's all I can hear, but exhaustion takes over, the darkness seems to swallow me as I attempt to focus on what they're say. Words twist together with every second passing. As much as I want to keep my eyes open, I can't.

I fight it, I pray to the darkness for my lashes to stay open, but the feeling is too strong. I allow it to take me over, to wash over me like a wave crashing on the shore. It's a peaceful feeling when death comes for you.

If they're here, then it means they managed to capture my father. It's the only thing I wanted—for him to pay. I know The Fallen will do what they need to when it comes to vengeance.

With the thought in mind, I allow my end of lull me into a sense of warmth. As if I'm lying on a soft pillow, I ignore the pain which ebbs away, trickling out of my body. Darkness holds me, it keeps me in its arms, much like Falcon, Crow, and Hawk have been there for me.

There is no longer a doubt in my mind—I've fallen for them. As I come to terms with my emotions, I allow myself to give into the strength and power of the shadows.

My lashes flutter, and I whisper a silent goodbye to the men who took me, stole me, and yet, showed me everything I am.

I now accept it.

Seconds later all I see is black.

Twenty Six
HAWK

ANGER.

It's all I feel when I see her broken body lying on the asphalt. I left the guys behind to deal with Mahoney when Drake and Dante broke in with their team. There was no longer any question in my mind this woman was ours.

I spent my life seeing people hurt. Watching innocents bleed out in front of you changes your perspective. I hated her for so long, I realize I was holding onto the emotions her father awoke inside me.

Lucille is innocent.

She's one of the souls we have sworn to protect. Even Crow has admitted she's ours. It makes me the only one of us who has been struggling with

263

admitting the truth.

"How is she?" Drake asks as he stops beside us. He's drenched in blood.

"Not good, can you take her to the house? I need to help them." I wouldn't trust anyone else with her. Our relationship with the Savage brothers has been ongoing, it's been strong. They haven't led us wrong yet.

"Of course," he tells me, and lifts Lucille into his arms. Jealousy roars in my ears when he takes her away, but I know it's for the best. Once he's gone, I hop in my car and speed through the streets which lead back to the farm. Thankfully, they didn't get far.

Once I pull up to the building, I find Crow and Falcon with Dante and Mahoney. The old bastard is chained to the rafters, hanging from thick metal cuffs. He doesn't seem perturbed at his predicament. But then again, I didn't expect him to be.

"Where is she?" Falcon is the first to ask. I don't doubt he loves her. Falcon has always been the more emotional of the three of us. As The Fallen, we've allowed pain to hide the affection we may have to offer, but with Lucille, he's struggled to ignore his feelings.

"She's safe."

Mahoney laughs out loud. The sound captures my attention, it holds me hostage much the same as when he stole my sister. He first however, made her cry. The sound of his grunts, and the gentle whimpers of her pain stabs right through my chest.

"You're all boys," he spits, "Thinking someone like her can want you. Love you. Do you realize she is nothing more than a whore for rent?"

His words incite violence, and Crow is the first to wield his knife. The blade slicing into the thigh of our captive. "If you speak about her like that, make no mistake, you will die before she has a moment to get her revenge."

"She loves me," he tells Crow. "She always has, even when she was real little she loved her daddy." His words send ice through my veins and bile rises up slowly into my mouth. The acidic burn reminds me I'm alive and my sister isn't.

It's my turn. I step forward, pulling out the item I kept hidden in my jacket pocket all night. None of the men found it because they didn't think anything of it. The small round ball is made of metal, but they didn't realize once the lock latches at the back of the head, a blade shoots out, slicing through the tongue.

I move closer to Mahoney, and smile. I haven't offered anyone a grin in so long it feels fake, but with him, it's a reminder of what he's about to lose. I bind the leather around his neck while the ball slips between his teeth.

The moment the metal teeth clasp together, the blade shoots out. Blood splutters from Mahoney's lips. Crimson dripping from his chin, soaking the perfectly white shirt he's still wearing.

"You will never live to see her bask in the glory of your death," I tell him. "You may think you've won, but you have lost far more than you can imagine."

Falcon takes a step forward. "We're taking him to the bunker," he informs me, and I smirk. When we get him home, this bastard will rue the day he was born. I nod. Falcon glances behind me, and orders, "Take him down, we'll leave now."

I didn't ever expect to want to save the girl, but there's nothing I want more. She's ours and I'm not letting her out of my sight. I've spent most of the time hiding from her, I needed time to figure out why she has such an effect on me. But now I know why, she experienced the same abuse I did at the hands of her father.

"We need to get to her," I tell Falcon as they drag Mahoney away.

Dante steps forward, his hand offered in greeting. "My men will bring Mahoney to your house. Go to her, I know Drake will look after her until you get there." Even though it's the first time I've met this man, I know he's good. But I do recognize the darkness inside him.

We don't waste time getting back to the house. When I step inside, I make my way to Lucille's bedroom. She's sitting up in bed, and Drake is talking to her, but stops the moment he hears me enter the room.

"Are you okay?" My focus is on Lucille. The footsteps of my brothers follow me inside, and we make our way to the bed.

"A little banged up. Lost consciousness but Drake watched over me," she whispers, a small smile offered to Drake which only makes me jealous once more. This girl is making me crazy. I've never been a jealous person. I didn't expect to care for her as much as I do. But now she's in our lives, I can't deny I don't want to lose her.

"Thank you," I tell our friend.

"I know what it's like to lose the woman you love," he says, and it's the first time I ever thought about *that* word. It's never been in my vocabulary. The emotion hasn't been present in my mind, or my chest for years. Not since I lost my sister. But now he's said it, I glance at Lucille and nod.

"You need a doctor," Crow announces, and pulls his phone from his pocket. He leaves the room, holding the cell to his ear, and I turn my focus back to Lucille.

"We have Mahoney," I tell her. I still can't bring myself to admit my feelings. It's difficult to say the words. Those I've never said to anyone. No woman in my life has ever made me feel.

"I-Is he here?"

I nod. "Down in the bunker, we'll take you to see him once you're healed." Her eyes brim with unshed tears, and as much as I want to wipe them away, I also enjoy seeing them shimmer in her golden eyes.

I've fought it for so long, but the need to take her, to keep her, it's overwhelming. "I'm going to check on everything. Falcon will stay with you," I tell her before pushing to my feet and glancing at my brother. He offers me a knowing smirk, and I want nothing more than to roll my eyes. He told both Crow and me we'll succumb to the beauty, but I didn't believe it. Not only for myself, but for Crow as well.

When I reach the hallway, I see him ending the call. "She's okay?"

"Yeah." We walk together as we make our way down to the stairs which will lead us to our prisoner. I can't believe we finally have him. It's been too easy. Everything was far too fucking easy.

"Do you think he wanted to be caught?" Crow's question lingers in my mind. Perhaps he did. But there will never be a way to know for sure. He's nothing more than a liar, so even if we were to ask, it wouldn't be answered with the truth.

"If he did, why now? He's paid with his daughter's life for freedom. It doesn't make sense he would surrender so easily."

Suddenly, an explosion rumbles from the back of the house. I realize why the ease of how we captured Mahoney wasn't sitting well with me. They haven't given up. This is an onslaught. The front door is hammered in, the wood splintering, and shots ring in the air.

Crow and I fall to the ground, crawling toward the safety of the office and when we shut ourselves in, he makes a beeline for the safe which has weapons we can use to fight back. Windows shatter in the distance, and all I find myself praying for is Falcon and Lucille are safe.

I don't care about myself. I've witnessed enough horrors to last me a lifetime, so if for any reason I don't make it out alive, as long as they're okay.

"Get the fuck out of your head," Crow hisses when he nears me. He hands me a Glock, and I cock it before nodding, attempting to focus on the here and now. We have to fight back. I pull open the door and we slide against the wall, making our way back out to where there are men in black suits holding machine guns camped close to the exit. Crow takes the lead with the silencer and aims at the closest of the soldiers. He goes down instantly, and we continue our onslaught.

"They're going to take Mahoney," I whisper, and Crow cocks his head toward the basement.

"Go." I don't need to be told twice. I make my way down the stairs, taking them slow and steady. I don't know if they've reached the downstairs, but if they have, I need to be careful. My chest tightens as my heart thuds against my ribs.

It's silent.

That's never a good thing.

I wonder how they breached the house without the alarms tripping. When I finally get to the bunker, I find Mahoney still chained up. It's a low ceiling, which doesn't stretch his limbs as much as the warehouse would have, but it works.

"Who have you contacted?" I bite out before butting him in the mouth with the gun. Blood seeps from his lips, and when he grins at me, the crimson darkens his teeth, making him look sinister. The same smile he gave me *that* night.

"Your sister was so good," he tells me in a low grunt. "So fucking tight," he continues, and rage explodes in my vision. All I see is red. I hit him. Dropping the gun to the ground, I use my fists. My knuckles biting into his flesh as I make sure every hit is painful and raw. The violence coursing through my blood is addictive. It's why I fight. I wrap my fingers around his throat and squeeze.

"If you kill me, you'll never see her again," he tells me, causing me to halt all movement.

"What?"

270

He chuckles at my question. The shock on my face must be obvious as he pins me with a glare. "She is still alive. Working hard like she was born to."

"You're lying." I don't believe a fucking word he's saying. Even if I did, I can't allow him to fuck with my head. I'll find her myself. If she truly is alive somewhere in this world, I have connections who will be able to track her down. I was convinced she was dead. Perhaps it would have been better if she was because I can't imagine her living through the horrors girls who are sold face.

Not now, not ever.

"You can believe what you want," Mahoney tells me. "But the Cartel have links in every fucking country, and it doesn't matter what you do, there will always be a way for them to hide her. But I know where she is. Her exact location."

"If you don't tell me, I'll gut you like a fish and leave your entrails for the wild animals to eat." I grab a screwdriver from my table of toys I use on the men we bring down here and trail it along his face. "Now tell me, who is coming into our home, trying to kill us, and where the fuck is my sister?"

"Well, it will be me you're looking for," a deep baritone sounds behind me. Beside the man who looks like he should be in a boardroom not a damn basement is Lucille.

"What's going on?" I flick my gaze between them, taking in her guilty expression while noting Falcon and Crow behind them.

"It's okay," Crow tells me. "He's here for Mahoney."

"No." Mahoney struggles in his restraints. "I'm not going with him."

"Would you like to die here or back in Mexico?" The stranger asks, his dark glare pinned on the man chained up behind me.

Frustration burns through me because I have no fucking clue who he is, or why Crow and Falcon are willing to let this man take Mahoney. This is our vengeance, not his. "What the fuck is going on?"

"Lucille," the stranger says as her name rolls off his tongue. His eyes track hers, and it seems she knows who he is. My gut churns as she regards him with a smile.

"Hawk, I need you to listen to me, to trust me," she says, stepping forward. With every movement, I can see her hands tremble. "This man is here to help us," she says. "He can bring your sister back."

I flick my gaze to his. "Is this true?"

"I know where she is, yes. The twins as well," he tells us, glancing at Crow. "But I need to take Mahoney in. There's no other way. It will be a swap."

"Who the fuck are you?"

He pulls out his wallet and hands me a card.

Undercover agent. "I've been working on this case for almost eight years. It's the first time we could get Mahoney where we need him, out of prison so we can exact the correct punishment."

"No, I'm not going with anyone," the old bastard says, as if he has any choice in the matter. He will do as we please, not as he wants.

"Bring my sister and the twins," I tell Agent Ramirez. "We will talk."

Once he's gone, I know I need to talk to the guys. We need to figure this shit out. I didn't miss the fact Falcon's brother wasn't included in the deal.

Twenty Seven
CROW

We're seated in the living room with Lucille between Hawk and myself, and Falcon at her feet. The sight of us all cocooning her has him smiling. He's the gentle one, mostly. But after what she's been through, I have a feeling we're going to want to keep her close for a long while until she's not shaking like she is right now.

"Tell me what the fuck that was?" Hawk is frustrated. But when Ramirez walked in, I was holding a gun to his head. Shit had gone down, and they were convinced this was Mahoney's hideout. When I told him we had the bastard chained up downstairs, he called off his team.

"Ramirez is convinced he knows where Molly and the twins are. I don't know if they're alive, or if it's true, but I needed to make the decision. We all did." I glance at Lucille and Falcon. "If we can get them back, then we'll hopefully be able to heal our families. Who knows who else he has found. I mean, this could close a case which has been open for years. We don't know what we're going to do once we get confirmation it is our siblings, but it's worth a fucking shot."

"This Ramirez guy, you trust him?"

"As much as I can," I tell Hawk. "You know how much I hate cops, agents even more, but if he has intel, I'm willing to listen." I'm not the biggest fan of any law enforcement. The reason being when my brothers were taken, they didn't do their job. I believe they could have stepped up more than they did. It's why we lost them.

"I still don't like it," Hawk tells me. "What if he's here to free Mahoney again?"

The thought did cross my mind. "Which is why I asked for us to be present when they end him." When the agent explained his reasons for breaking into our home, I needed more than a promise. There had to be substantial reasoning for me to step back and allow him to take the man I spent half my life wanting to kill.

I would have happily gone to prison if I had taken out Mahoney with my bare hands. The satisfaction would have brought me closure. So, I made a deal. I struck it with Falcon and Lucille beside me. I should have waited for Hawk, but I knew he would've trusted me. Even if he didn't trust the cop.

"My father will be taken in by them and will pay for what he did," Lucille tells him. She's been through so much today, but the way her eyes sparkle makes my chest ache. She still looks at us, each of us, as if we're her saviors. When we're the ones who put her in this fucking mess. If it wasn't for me, she would never have been in the car with Volkov.

"It's a chance I'm willing to take," I tell Hawk.

His gaze flicks to Falcon. He's the only one of us who doesn't get his sibling back. Ramirez didn't mention anything about Falcon's brother. I can't imagine how many children these bastards have taken, and I don't want to think about what they've been through in the past ten or more years.

"What about you?" Hawk finally asks Falcon.

We all look over at him, and he offers a smile. "If we can get a handful back, it's a win in my book. I won't trust this asshole until I see evidence, or I see either the twins, or your sister," he says to Hawk.

"I have to agree," Hawk says with a nod. "I don't trust anyone until I see proof, living fucking proof."

"What about the revenge you need on my father?" Lucille asks.

"She's right," I murmur. "The thought of

walking away from something we worked so hard on for years, is tragic. I don't want to lose. I don't want to see him walk off without paying for what he did."

"Then perhaps we make him pay," Falcon says. "We don't have to kill him, but we can most definitely ensure he never hurts anyone ever again."

"What did you have in mind?" I smirk, thinking of all the ways we can do damage without killing the bastard.

"Why don't we each have a turn? Unless you want to watch?" Falcon questions, his face flicking to each of us. I don't think Lucille will want to be there when I take my turn. I'm going to make her father regret the day he was born.

"I want to see," she pipes up suddenly. "I want to see everything. I'm not some fragile little girl anymore." Her confidence is an aphrodisiac. I want her more than I ever expected to. She's here, claimed and owned by us, she's never leaving.

"Are you sure?" I ask, knowing whatever each of us have planned will not be pretty to watch. She's still innocent, mostly, compared to the rest of us. Lucille hasn't seen the darkness we have. As much as she thinks she has.

"Yes," her confidence brims through her eyes, shining like a star in the darkest night.

"Okay," I nod, moving to stand. I offer her a

hand and pull her to stand. "If you want to leave at any point, the door will be open."

Those golden orbs lock on mine, and her smile is infectious as she regards me. "I'm not leaving." Her words hold a deeper meaning. It's not only about the rest of this evening, it's about forever.

"Then we best get on with it," I tell her as I lead her, along with my brothers down to the basement. When we reach Mahoney, he's still holding on for dear life. There's no longer anything standing in my way. I leave Lucille at the entrance with Hawk and Falcon. "It's time to pay your penance," I say as I pick up a sharp, metal spoke. The thick steel is about ten inches long, and it's got tiny ridges on it which make it look like there are blades shooting off from the main spike.

"Do what you must," he bites out, his eyes on Lucille which only seems to incite violence inside me. My blood boils, races through my veins as I watch him look at her. I don't want any other man's eyes on my girl. Our girl.

I take the steel weapon and I slide it along his face, the crimson bursts from the tiny cuts looks like a pretty pattern of violence. I stop when I reach his crotch.

"This is for my brothers," I tell him as I round his hanging body and stop behind him. The slick metal slices through his suit pants until I hear the cries of agony from the man who needs to pay for his sins.

I smile when I see blood drenching his slacks. The deep crimson nothing more than a dye which darkens the material. "Does it feel good?" Falcon questions, his voice taking on a sinister tone. "Because we all known how much you wanted boys for your own violent desires."

I twist the weapon, the metal slicing through flesh. But then I notice the flick of a lighter, and Hawk has stepped forward. He holds the dancing flame to Mahoney's nose, the amber flicker singes hairs, and then, the stench of burning flesh violates my nostrils.

"This is for my sister," Hawk tells Mahoney. "Does it feel good?" The question is one I know to be Mahoney's signature. Most serial killers have a tell. It's how they become famous, and this was his. The gentle tone of his voice, asking the question as he violated multitudes of innocents.

The squirming agony emanates from our captive is what I'd always dreamed about. A metallic scent hangs in the air. Blood—it has the perfume of violence, and the fragrance of vengeance.

"I spent my life wanting this, craving it," I tell our victim. "Now it's here, it's better than I ever imagined."

Mahoney's gaze lifts to mine. He looks nothing

like this daughter. He's nothing like her and she doesn't take after him at all. She's kind, sweet, she enjoys seeing people smile. The man before me is a monster, and his own flesh and blood hasn't even captured those traits. He is nothing.

"She's a whore who will only end you in your sleep one day," he tells me. "Mark my words. Her darkness is equal to mine." Suddenly, Lucille appears from behind me, and she grabs one of the pliers which lie on the table and she shoves it into his chest. Blood spurts from the wound, but I no longer care if he dies in our care. Ramirez will have to deal with it.

I will see my brothers again if they're alive. But right now, we all need this. It's Hawk who steps up last, taking his place beside Falcon. Both men are livid. Their eyes are wild with violence.

A sleek leather belt is wrapped around Mahoney's neck, and slowly, Hawk tightens his hold. Veins bulge in the older man's throat, and I can't help but smile. Lucille leans into me, and I know she must be exhausted. Hawk's mouth is right at the man's ear.

"Did you like it rough?" The question is a whisper, before Falcon takes a blade from the table and he slices into Mahoney's cheek.

My nostrils burn with the knowledge we're getting what we always wanted. The vengeance of

The Fallen has taken place, and we will be able to sleep easier tonight. It's only taken a girl coming into our lives to bring this to us.

Lucille may have been part of the plan, but she easily earned her place as part of The Fallen. I wanted so badly to see her cry, to watch her feel the pain we did, but she was never guilty.

Even when I believed she was, it was Falcon who urged me to look through my anger. It's who I am, when rage fills me, it also fuels me. I act on sight, rather than wait to see what comes from the puzzle as it falls apart.

We watch as Mahoney passes out from the pain. His burnt flesh fills the basement with a vile stench. The blood on the other hand seems to calm me somewhat.

"Ramirez will be back," I tell them, "Let's get our girl to bed." We move to the door, leaving our prisoner hanging by his wrists. It's time to move on now. We've gotten what we needed.

Granted, it would have been better to kill the man. But if keeping him alive means we get to see our siblings again, I'm all for it. We move silently through the house. The door is still broken, but the alarm is set. If anyone sets foot on the property, we'll know.

We have a few hours before agents once more descend on our home. In the morning, I'm going to make sure to get the damn door fixed. The cold is no joke in the middle of winter. As we step into my bedroom, I realize it's almost Christmas.

"Undress and get under the covers," I tell Lucille, releasing her from my hold. Falcon helps her while Hawk and I stand back. Watching him fuss over Lucille makes me smile. He's always been the more attentive of us but seeing him care for her does things to me. It brings out emotions I don't want to admit to.

Falcon helps her into bed. The fact she's in my bed, in her panties and nothing else doesn't help the raging need to devour her. The moment her head hits the pillow, her lashes flutter. The three of us watch her for a long time. We stand side by side and take in our Goldilocks. She may not have stolen our beds, but she definitely stole our fucking hearts.

Epilogue
CROW

H<small>E CAME THROUGH. T</small>HE CAR IS PULLING UP TO THE house right now and I don't know whether I want to laugh or cry. It sounds stupid, but knowing I'm going to see my brothers again, sets me on edge. I don't know what they've been through or where they've been living, but at least they're alive.

When the car doors swing open, I take in the agents who exit first. Last night, I spent most of it awake, wondering if this is truly happening. As two young men step out of the vehicles, I'm speechless.

They're all grown up. Men. No longer boys. No longer children. They look around, taking in the house before their gazes land on me. Twins. They were always so alike in everything they did. Even their schoolwork was mimicked.

283

"Joshua? James?" Their names feel foreign on my tongue. As if I'm talking to strangers. As if I'm regarding them for the first time ever. In some ways, I am. In other ways, they're the same. There's nothing different except the fact they're taller. Broader. They have filled out.

"Cordon?"

I don't know how to respond, but when both of them rush toward me, and slam into me, I can't stop the tears from falling from my eyes. Emotion. It's choking me the more they hold onto me as if I'm their lifeline. I'm not, but I'm fucking crying when they look up at me, and smile.

"It's you," Josh says, his voice a cracked whisper drenched in pain. "I didn't think we would ever see you again."

I can't speak. I can't find words to express how I feel. James steps back and grins. "Old man," he says. "I've missed you." It was his nickname for me when we were younger. Before all the shit happened.

"Come," I tell him, leaving the agents to deal with Mahoney. "It's time you met your family." Our folks aren't here right now, but they need to learn about who I am, and the people who stood beside me all these years.

I know Hawk will be waiting for Missy, so I let him have his privacy. The boys seem calm, relaxed even, but I don't doubt there will be more to it than smiles and them trying to joke about being gone.

When we step into the house, Lucille is standing there waiting. She's dressed in a black pants and jacket, with a white blouse, which makes her look like a lawyer. The long black pants hits her ankles, and it dips and peaks on her curves. A gentle hint of cleavage is peeking through. She's never looked classier.

"I need you to meet Lucille," I tell them. We decided to wait until we're all settled and used to each other before they learn who her father is. Hatred can run deep, I'm an expert in knowing about how much emotion can eat away at your soul.

I want them to love her. She's mine and she will be their sister in law.

"Hi," James says, taking Lucille's hand and shaking it. "I'm the handsomer brother," he tells her. I want to know how he's so calm, so *normal*, but I don't ask right now.

"I'm Joshua, but you can call me Josh," he says with a grin which belies what he must have been through.

"It's nice to meet you both," Lucy tells them. "I'm glad you're here, Crow has been worried about you both."

"Cordon?" Josh glances at me, his eyes shine with questions which I can't give answers to.

"We need to talk," I tell them, "Go to your room,

little mouse," I say to my girl. "I'll come get you later." She obeys without question. It's been months and she's gotten used to me, used to us, and she's become more submissive which only seems to make my blood heat with desire.

"What's going on?" Josh asks once we're alone. I turn, gesturing for them to follow me. When we reach my office, I shut the door behind them and watch as they settle on the sofa. Both flopping like teenagers on the soft leather.

"What happened to you both?" The question is out of my mouth before I can fully consider the answers they'll give. I don't know if I want to know, but I need to. I join them, my focus on the two boys who are now grown men.

"Strangely enough, we were looked after," Josh says. "We lived with this guy who fed us, bought us clothes. He didn't want anything from us."

"Yeah," James reiterates. "We lived lavish for a while."

I glance between them, meeting Joshua's eyes, I ask, "What was his name?"

"We knew him as Boss Man. But we do know he was mafia," my brother tells me. "Italian mafia. We were in Italy for the past five years."

"I don't—"

I'm interrupted by James, "He took us on as if we were family. I don't know if he was working for the feds, but the agent who brought us home knew him. It was as if they were friends, or something."

I realize there is more to the story. I'm almost certain, Missy has to be the one to shed some light.

* * *

HAWK

Seeing her again has my heart soaring. She's alive. She's well. I didn't think she would be breathing, but here she is right in front of me. Missy looks at me as if in shock. She doesn't look hurt, but I can tell the light which used to shine in her eyes has been dimmed. When she falls into my arms, her body trembles, and I feel all the darkness I held onto for so long crack.

The walls I built up over the years are slowly crumbling, and it's all because my sister is home. She is warm against me, her tears soaking through the material of my shirt. But I can't let go. I squeeze her tighter, and I breathe in the clean scent of her hair. The long, dark strands hang in waves, and when she looks up at me again, her green eyes shimmer.

"I never thought I'd see you again," she whispers, her lips shake as emotion takes a hold of her.

"I'm always here for you," I tell her. "All you have to worry about now is telling me exactly what happened to you. I need to know everything."

She nods as I lead her into the lounge where Falcon is sitting with Crow and the twins. They're all grown up now. When their eyes lock on Missy, I want to hide her away. No boys, or men, should be looking at my little sister. But she's not young anymore, she's almost eighteen.

"Missy," Crow greets her, and she offers a soft *hello,* and one to Falcon. She doesn't look at the twins, and I'm thankful for that. I wouldn't want to kill them only as Crow got them back.

We settle in and Lucille joins us moments later. I watch my sister. She's so different to what I remember. Grown up.

"I was taken to a boat, for weeks," she says. "In the dark, I spent time with a few other girls who were the same age as me. We didn't know what was happening. I'm not sure how much time had passed when they pulled us up and took us to some gathering on the deck of this huge boat."

"Did you see anyone you recognized?" Crow asks before I have time to do so.

Missy shakes her head, "No. Not even the girls were familiar to me. They lined us up, stripped us down, and we were told to be quiet. Men walked up, touched us," she whispers, and her voice breaks as her emotion trickles down her cheeks. "One of the girls fought back and they killed her right in front of us."

"Jesus," Falcon hisses, his anger palpable. "You were auctioned?"

Missy nods. "Yes," she says. "I was sold for five million."

"What was his name?" If she can remember, we can get more information on what the fuck happened to her. "Where were you?"

"The man was French. There were Italians as well, but they took other girls. But the one who bought me was royalty or something. His house was in the hills of south France. I... I..." Her words falter, and I wonder why she can't speak.

What the fuck did she go through that's hurt her so much?

"I loved him," she admits and my body grows cold. It's as if ice is running through my veins. "I really did." When Missy looks at me, I see it in her eyes. She believes this man was good. But how? He *bought* her.

"You mean you didn't want to come home?"

"No, I did. I mean, I just..." She shakes her head as if regret is settling in her gut, her mouth pursed as she ponders her next words. "I missed you all, but he wouldn't let me leave. But he was a good man."

"No man who buys a child is good," I bite out,

rage fueling me once more. I've spent my life living with anger.

But when Missy looks at me again, she smiles. "He didn't touch me, didn't hurt me. He cared for me." The way she's talking doesn't help my anger. "I don't know why, or how, but I was happy. For a time. The agents came to talk to him, they explained they were undercover and needed his help. They wanted me in exchange for his freedom, immunity. He took it. He let me go so he could walk free."

"And you want this man free?" This comes from Falcon, the shock in his voice mimics the surprise I'm feeling.

"Yes," Missy says. Then looks at me. "Promise me you won't do anything. I'm home now. I'm safe. I won't leave again, but please, Mikhail," she pleads, using my real name. I haven't heard it in so long, it feels strange, foreign. "Promise me."

I don't know how to say yes, to vow I won't find and kill this man, but for my sister, I'll find it in myself, deep in my soul, to gift her this. "Sure."

I don't know what's going to happen in the future, but right now, all I want is my family.

All I need is to hold everyone closer because you never know when they'll be gone.

Epilogue
LUCILLE

Six months later

M<small>Y CAPTORS HAVE BECOME MY SAVIORS. I DIDN'T EXPECT</small> to *want* to stay with them. But I do. After watching my father die, I've become accustomed to the fact his life needed to come to an end. There were no more apologies needed.

Crow, Falcon, and Hawk got the vengeance they craved. I'm proud of myself for allowing it to happen. He was after all, my father. My blood. But now he's no longer in the world, I know I'll be okay.

Yes, there is darkness inside me, but it's satiated by the new life I found. Three men have taken me under their wing. Safety has never been something I could claim I felt, not after I learned who my father was and what he did to me. But with The Fallen, I'm home.

There were times over the past few months where I wondered if I would ever be okay with who I am. For years, I hid the darkness. I ignored it, shoved it into the back of my mind. But now I've learned how to feed it, how to tame it, I'm no longer afraid.

"Is this where you're hiding?" Hawk enters the library, and I glance over my shoulder to see him saunter in wearing a pair of jeans, with a tight fitting white tee. The muscles of his chest and arms bunch and release with every movement, and I can't deny, he's beautiful.

He was the last one of the three to accept me. But now he has, we've grown so much closer. I've learned more about him. Knowing he tried to go to war to forget what my father had done to him made me sad. It felt as if he was forced into a new life, one he didn't want because of the trauma.

"I needed to think about the future," I tell him. When I told them I wanted to go study, to try something new, all three were ready to pack up their lives and move with me. But I couldn't ask them to do that.

Crow made it clear I will never be able to leave The Fallen. I was one of them now. As much as I do love them, I realized I had to find my own way without the fear of what could happen if my father ever found me.

"You know what your future holds," Hawk says as he settles into an armchair across from me. His legs crossed at the angle, making him look like a lounging tiger, waiting for me to make a move.

"I can't—"

"If you try to leave us, you know we'll find you. We will follow you anywhere you go," he informs me of something I already knew. There's no doubt in my mind these men have already stalked me, they had already knew everything there was to know about me. I had no idea who they were.

"What if I were to come back after?"

"Do you really want to leave?" he challenges. "Because if you do, we'll allow it for a short time, but you have to remember there is no way Crow and Falcon will accept it." He's right, so I can't argue with him. They will lose their shit if I were to leave. They've both made it clear.

"What about you?" As much as I know Hawk accepts me, and enjoys me in their home, he's never admitted how he feels about me. He's never said those three words, the ones I want to hear. That I ache to hear.

When I was younger, I never thought I would want a man to love me. But now, having to who do, Hawk means so much to me, I want him to admit it as well.

His eyes shimmer as he regards me. "You've tempted me since the moment you stepped into my life. When you bumped into me that night, I couldn't deny I craved you. There were no words to describe how deeply I hungered to taste you on my tongue, to feel you on my lips. But I don't do emotions."

"I never did for a long time," I tell him. "But then you, Crow, and Falcon came along." It's no longer embarrassing to admit I want them. I don't feel shame when I think about how they feed my demons, how they satisfy the darkness residing in my soul. "But I need *that*," I tell him, keeping the emphasis on the last word.

Hawk regards me for a long, silent moment. When he finally breaks into a gentle smile, he nods. "I understand," he says as he pushes to his feet, offering his hands for to me to take a hold of and I accept. He pulls me up, and brings me into his arms, as they wrap around me like a cocoon. I nestle into his warmth.

"I'm sorry," I tell him, unsure of why I'm apologizing. He doesn't need it from me, not anymore. But I can't help saying because I know he was affected deeply by what happened. Knowing how my father tortured him still niggles at the back of my mind.

"Lucille," Hawk says as he steps back and cups my face in his hands. His hold on me calming, but his eyes dance with affection. "I didn't think it would ever be possible, but I do." He doesn't say the words, and he chuckles when I roll my eyes. "I love you," he tells me with a smile, and I can't help but sink into him again.

"You two are so adorable." Falcon's voice comes from behind me, but I don't release my hold on Hawk. "I kind of feel sick with all the goddamned sweetness in this room right now." The heat of him at my back sandwiches me between the two firm bodies. "But I know how to make things right." His voice rumbles against me, the vibration sending pleasure through every part of me. From head to toe, I'm calm, I'm safe.

"Oh?" I arch a brow looking at him from over my shoulder. "How on earth do you expect to do that?" I ask him, a small smile curling my lip. There's a sly glint in his eye as he regards me.

His hands trail down my sides causing me to shiver while Hawk holds me tight. I can't move. I can't escape, and I realize, I really don't want to.

* * *

FALCON

Fuck, she does things to me. Seeing her with Crow or Hawk, it makes my blood turn hot with desire. The idea of having her here forever makes my heart soar. I may have been the first of us who accepted her. While Hawk was the last, I can tell he's finally admitted his feelings. He has always been less open about how his emotions have taken a hold of him.

"Kiss him," I coo in Lucille's ear, my breath fanning over her cheek and she shivers in response. "I want to watch you be a filthy girl," I tell her, before rolling my hips, allowing her to feel my hardness. Desire runs hot in my blood and takes over, and I know our Goldilocks will enjoy being amongst the three of us the way she always does.

Crow is on his way down, and when he does get here, I can't imagine what he's going to find. I want her naked. Slowly, I tease the tank top she's wearing down over her shoulders and I allow it to dip under her breasts.

Hawk's gaze is burning a hole through the both of us as he leans in and steals her lips. Their kiss, their tongues tangle as I smile. The sight is an aphrodisiac which only makes my dick jolt with the need to be inside her. I want her filled up.

I can picture her taking each one of us, as we

enjoy each other. Sharing came to me easily, when it was with Crow and Hawk, I knew I would always want them in my life. I didn't think we would find a girl who would accept us, and then Lucy came along, and now, I couldn't be more satisfied.

Hawk glances at me, as he drops to his knees before her. I hold her steady as he tugs her joggers from her hips. She's not wearing any panties, and Hawk leans in to lap at her cunt which has her wobbling on her feet.

Soft whimpers fall from her lips as I help her settle back on my lap. She wiggles her cute ass as she teases my dick with her movements.

"If you keep that up, I'm going to be balls deep in your tight little ass," I warn her, which only makes her do it even more. But, Hawk, along with my help, moves both her legs on either side of mine so she's spread open for him.

With one hand on my balls, and the other on her mound, his mouth lands on her cunt, and Lucille and I both watch him lick at her tight little hole which is now dripping wet. His face is drenched in her sweet juices.

The scent of sex fills the room as her arousal glistens on Hawk's chin. I can't deny I'm jealous. "I want you both," he tells us as he looks up at us from his kneeling position between her thighs. I shove my joggers down, until my hard dick pops free, and slaps against Lucille's wet cunt.

The sounds of her pleasure echo around us. It's a symphonic, melodic, and intoxicating. I want to listen to her all day every day. There's nothing I wouldn't do for her, and I know Crow and Hawk are in the same mindset.

It's taken us time to get there, but we're here right now and feeling her body tremble and shake confirms she's as lost in this pleasure as we are. I didn't expect to ever feel this way about a woman before. But with her, it's easy.

I love my brothers, but I also love Lucille. She's beauty personified. She's lust and desire, passion and need. The darkness in her overwhelms me at times, the same way Crow's shadows do, but I will happily bask in them if it means I get to keep them both.

Our bodies are in sync. We're no longer four people enjoying sex, we're one.

He grips my dick and strokes it against his. They look obscene, but when Hawk looks up at Lucille, I know exactly what's going through his mind.

"Are you ready, Goldilocks?" he questions, his eyes holding all the power as he keeps her gaze hostage. Lucille nods as she leans back against my chest and I watch in awe as our cocks disappear from sight. The tightness is nothing like I Ever experienced, and as Lucille slowly slips down both

298

our shafts, my eyes roll back in my head.

Crow's grunt is loud, but I can't focus on anything other than our girl taking both Hawk and I in her tight little pussy. The way she moans is nothing short of filth. She sounds like a whore, a slut enjoying being broken by men. It's what she is when she's lost in the darkness with us.

Soft gagging sounds echo around us as she swallows Crow with all she has. Her throat works around his dick while her cunt pulses around two cocks at the same time. It's too fucking much and I have to bite down on my lip to keep from cumin.

The sensation of Hawk's wet cock sliding against mine sends me into orbit as we fuck Lucille until she's screaming out loud. Her tight, wet walls pulse around us, and I know there is no going back now. This woman owns us as much as we claimed her.

When we're all satiated, the only thing makes sense is for us all to nestle amongst each other in the super king-sized bed in Crow's bedroom.

We can worry about logistics tomorrow.

* * *

Thank You
ACKNOWLEDGMENTS

For my first RH, I have to say this was quite a ride. I loved every minute of it, so there may be more in the future. ;) I hope you all fell in love with my boys—Crow, Falcon, and Hawk.

I huge thank you to Amy Briggs for helping me last minute with edits. You are a lifesaver!

To my PA, Caroline, as always, thank you for being the adult and making sure I get shit done.

To my readers, the amazing ladies in my reader group, The Deviants, thank you for always being so incredible, and to my Captive Angels for pimping my ass out, you ladies ROCK!

To all the bloggers, bookstagrammers, and booktokers, I hope that as my first RH romance, I've done it justice and you enjoyed it. Thank you for always taking time out of your busy lives to help support and promote me. You are incredible.

Mad love,
Dani xo

Other books
BY DANI

For a full list of Dani René's incredible titles
visit her website www.danirene.com
or find her on all major retailers.

About
DANI

Dani is a *USA Today* Bestselling Author of seductive and deviant romance.

Her books range from the dark to emotional, but every hero is alpha, and each heroine is strong-willed, bringing the men down to their knees.

She now lives in the UK, after moving from Cape Town, exploring cemeteries and old buildings while plotting her next book.

When she's not writing, she can be found binge-watching the latest TV series, or working on graphic design. She has a healthy addiction to reading, tattoos, coffee, and ice cream.

www.danirene.com
info@danirene.com